雅思寫作聖經

大作文

Amanda Chou ◎ 著

QRCODE DOWNLOAD 英式發音

照著百搭「單句」＋「段落」套句
依樣葫蘆 轉瞬成為英寫高手

緊扣官方核心必考話題，任何話題撰寫均得心應手

補強課堂寫作盲點，並輔以大量段落中譯英練習，**活化思路、迅速組織**出7.5以上大作文高分實力。

精選高分範文並錄音，雙管齊下練「聽」＋「寫」，學習效果倍增

聽、寫**雙效強化**，相輔相成內建**百變句型**，**高分論點**均源源而至，時限內成竹在胸完成一篇英文佳作。

作者序

　　英文寫作能力的養成是需要長時間累積培養的。英文寫作的高分所涉及的部分非常廣泛，包含了對文法和句型的掌握和內容豐富性等等，而對於雅思寫作考試的設計，又以四個主要的評分項目為依歸，當中包含了「承轉詞的掌握和文章的一致性和連貫性」、「充分理解題目和完成任務回答」、「字詞的使用」和「語法使用和準確性」。在這些範疇中能討論的部分相當廣，而對大多數考生來說即使具備一定程度語法的掌握，仍可能僅考取雅思寫作 6.5 分，因為當中還涉及了很多原因和備考準備。

　　外文系寫作課程和坊間雅思補習當中確實有極富教學熱情的老師，細心地批改學生每篇英文作文，甚至在許多考生或學生的每篇作文中，幾乎在每個句子都能看到批改出的錯誤，包含了許多基礎的文法和細節上的批改。一學期的英文寫作課，如果是很密集、強度很高的寫作課程，在 18 週當中，每週要求考生要寫一篇 300 字的英文作文（一學期共 18 篇），都悉心指導和批改了，學生的進步卻仍非常有限，更何況是有些寫作課一學期只寫了幾篇（這部分其實還涉及了師生比和老師教學

熱誠等因素，在此就不探討了）。這些訊息都跟這本書的規劃設計是息息相關的。只單純仰賴教師批改且觀看錯在哪裡的學習方式，仍是太被動式的學習。學習者儘管都知道了「錯」在哪裡，仍可能在應考時又寫下了同樣的句子或發生誤用，考生並未因為教師的批改後就迅速修正了錯誤，無形中讓這些教師的費心指點化為流水。

對此，考生要採取的是更主動的學習模式，即主動修正並提高這些學習成效。在具備這樣的基礎後，再動筆寫一篇英文作文，因為這時候已經具備一定的語法能力。教師才更能針對英文作文的邏輯、連貫性和內容等給予建議，而非反覆批改 10 篇考生都重複錯的語句，例如：動名詞當主詞時，主要動詞要用單數或是可數名詞前面要加冠詞。這些細微的文法錯誤，可以在數篇作文中反覆不斷地改到，甚至在一篇作文中改出數十個類似的錯誤。書籍中所規劃的大量「單句中英互譯」就能迅速修正這點。俗話說：要先能寫好一個語法正確的句子，才能動筆寫一篇文章。其實能寫好一個句子就非常難了，因為每句的意思不同，使用到的句型不同，其所搭配的慣用語等亦不同。此外，還有英文時態等更多

衍生的問題存在。

　　所以，如果是修了數個學期英文寫作課或補習後，雅思寫作分數仍未顯著提升的考生，相信可以先從書中的單句中英互譯作為一個開端，並搭配坊間文法書合用。在具備這樣的基礎後，再開始撰寫文章，方能從中受益寫出文情並茂、論點具說服力的文章。另外，書中也規劃了「段落中譯英」，進一步強化考生的核心表達能力。這些段落都以在實際考試中能獲取 7.5 以上分數的語句編寫而成的，因為「百搭」所以考生在面對龐大的寫作考試話題上都能有所發揮、穩操勝卷。除此之外，考生一定要親自撰寫近幾年的所有雅思官方寫作題目，並確實記錄寫作時間。如果對備考仍不放心的考生，可以背誦本書中所收錄的大作文範文，並組織出自己的高分答題範文。最後祝所有考生都獲取理想成績。

Amanda Chou 敬上

使用說明

INSTRUCTIONS

▶ UNIT 31 模擬試題（三十一）

❶ Because of multiple YouTubers' remarks about the new product, some consumers remain hesitant, thinking that they have to wait until the doubt is cleared up.

❷ Shoppers cannot let go of the snide comments made by bloggers, so they have made up their minds to unsubscribe a certain channel.

❸ Although the notoriety of the masseur has been widely known in the neighborhood, tourists traveling here are still kept in the dark.

❹ Due to a lack of evidence and recordings at the scene, the authenticity of the bad service made by the bank clerk cannot be verified.

❺ Despite the fact that the CFO of the Best Consulting firm has done numerous buy-ins of the stocks before, he still cannot say for sure whether the bet can truly generate hefty profits.

140

❶ 因為許多 YouTuber 對該新產品的評論，有些消費者對其仍舊持著猶豫的態度，認為必須要等到疑慮消除為止。

❷ 購物者們無法甩脫由部落客們所做的惡意評論，所以他們已經下定決心要退訂特定的頻道。

❸ 儘管男按摩師的惡名昭彰在整個街坊已經是廣為人知，到此地旅遊的觀光客們卻仍被蒙在鼓底。

❹ 由於缺乏現場的證據和記錄，銀行行員服務差的真實性是無法證實的。

❺ 儘管倍斯特顧問公司的財務長已經於之前從事過為數眾多的股市買賣，他對於投注的賭注是否能真的產生鉅額的獲利仍無法說準。

141

Part 1 單句中英互譯

Part 2 段落中譯英

Part 3 精選大作文

中英雙向互譯、狂練 660 句（課堂或自學均適用）：
· 單句互譯可以用於高中和大學英語、寫作和翻譯課中，且可藉由中英對照規劃分組演練中譯英或英譯中，迅速提升寫作實力，單句互譯的單元演練後，學習者更具備寫作基礎實力。教師更易指導學生和減少花費在語法批改上的時間。

學習零障礙、學習規劃恰到好處：
· 獨家設計各程度均適用的學習法，由「單句」、「段落」、「整篇作文」循序漸進，由學習者和教師評估程度多元搭配學習，提升學習信心，鞏固核心寫作能力。

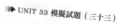

▶▶ UNIT 33 模擬試題（三十三）

❶ The lockdown of the city for a month has led to zero productivity and serenity of the street that are not usually seen in years.

❷ During the time of the outbreak of COVID-19 virus, bad things, such as layoffs and plant closure have become a regular scene.

❸ Singers and marine mammals are recruited to make the wedding more memorable and diverse, and the newlywed seems happy.

❹ Kitchen orders are usually enormous during the holiday, but with the invasion of the alien species, they are not as large as it used to be.

❺ Our fruits and vegetables are under such an extensive care that they are put in an artificial setting where temperatures are rigorously monitored.

148

Unit 33 模擬試題（三十三）

❶ 封城一個月已經導致生產力歸零且街道的寧靜是這幾年來不尋常的景象。

❷ 在新冠肺炎病毒爆發的期間，壞事例如解雇和工廠結束營業已經成了常景。

❸ 歌手們和海洋哺乳類動物都受僱，讓婚宴更有回憶性且多樣化，而新婚夫妻對此似乎感到樂此不疲。

❹ 在假日期間，廚房的訂單通常很大筆，但是隨著外來種的入侵，訂單沒有往常那麼多了。

❺ 我們的水果和蔬菜受到那樣的完善照護以致於它們被放置於溫度受到嚴密監控的人工環境裡。

Part 1 單句中英互譯

Part 2 段落中譯英

Part 3 精選大作文

149

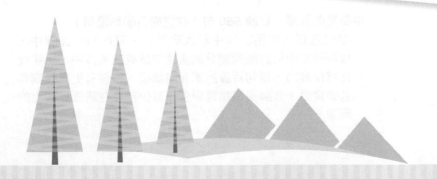

UNIT 44 漁業捕撈、「自生自滅」

段落中譯英迹 ▶ MP3 044

這些殘酷、不人道的漁業捕撈現象，其中一個例子就是對於鯊魚的迫害。在某些地區，人們捕抓鯊魚，並當場將鰭割下，因為這些鰭是鯊魚身上最獲利的部位，但更糟的是，這些鯊魚之後就被丟回深海裡，這實在可說是人類對於其他生物剝削手段的極致案例之一了，因為這些失去鰭的鯊魚，也失去了他們在其原本棲息的深海裡生存的能力，所以本質上來說，他們根本就是被棄置在深海裡自生自滅、等待死亡；若要有效地杜絕這類對海底生物的剝削手段，政府及國際組織應當同心協力，一同防止漁業過度捕撈的現象再度發生。

【參考答案】

One of these cruel and inhumane practices employed by some in the fishing industry includes the treatment of sharks. In certain regions, sharks are caught and their fins are cut off on the spot. What's worse, as the fins are the most valuable part on the body of sharks, many of those sharks are tossed right back into the deep sea. This is probably one of the purest forms of exploitation on these creatures as the sharks are essentially left to die when stripped of fins in the sea, unable to swim. To effectively bring this kind of exploitation to an end, governments and international organizations should work together to prevent overfishing from happening ever again.

段落翻譯中納入「邏輯申論」強化，
迅速組織出連貫語句：

· 提升「一致性和連貫性」單項成績，巧妙加強組織訊息和段落拓展實力，從臨摹到自己具備寫作出嚴密無倫文句的實力，一次就考取 7.5 分以上寫作高分。

段落翻譯和大範文均錄音，內建超語感：

· 由「聽」輔助「寫」＋「說」的學習，用零碎時間反覆
聽誦，腦海中閃現的片段字句逐步深印於腦，即學即用，
運用在各項英語考試中，並提升各英語測驗選擇題答題
實力。

UNIT 46　「謀事在人，成事在天」、「雙刃劍」

段落中譯英 ▶ MP3 046

　　換句話說，今日的癌症病患，正如「謀事在人，成事在天」所說，
必須學會如何接受，並不輕易放棄，堅強、持續與病魔奮鬥。以現有各
式各樣的癌症治療法來說，化療也許是治療上最常見的，而其療效也常
被認為具有所謂的「雙刃劍」效果，因為化療不只殺滅癌症細胞，同一
時間也對正常、良性的細胞造成衝擊，而因為有太多這些無法控制的變
因，癌症病患有時會因療程的不確定性感到氣餒，進而對治療感到憂
鬱、悲觀。

_____

_____

_____

_____

_____

【參考答案】

In other words, Today's cancer patients have to come to terms with the fact that all they can do is to remain positive and do not stop fighting, just as the saying "man proposes, God disposes" goes. In terms of cancer treatments that are currently available, there are a variety of options. Among these options, chemotherapy is probably the most common one in practice, and this therapy is often considered to be the sort of double edged sword treatment where not only cancer cells are destroyed through the treatment, but also the normal, good ones. Because of the fact that too many uncontrollable variables at stake, cancer patients can sometimes be discouraged by the uncertainty of the treatment and eventually become depressed and pessimistic.

諾貝爾和平獎得主，他曾說「成功不是達到幸福的關鍵。幸福才是達到成功的關鍵。」

_____

【參考答案】
My opinion resonates with Albert Schweitzer's famous saying. Albert Schweitzer, the recipient of the Nobel Peace Prize in 1952, once said, "Success is not the key to happiness. Happiness is the key to success."

❸ 將熱誠轉化為行動能帶來成就感。反之，只有錢並不能保證幸福；充其量這只是華而不實，遲早會崩解的成功表相。

_____

【參考答案】
Actualizing passion into action will induce a sense of fulfillment; instead, merely owning money is no guarantee for felicity; at best, it's a meretricious facade of success that will disintegrate sooner or later.

高分範文搶先看 ▸ MP3 056

In a capitalist society, owning a large amount of wealth seems to be the prime sign of success. Popular culture **exalts** the rich so much so that the rich have become the new royalty. Yet, if one **delves** into the **constituents** of success, he is likely to discover that money alone can hardly satisfy those elements, which is why I disagree with the statement.

My firm belief is that whether one has passion for what he does is the key. My opinion **resonates** with Albert Schweitzer's famous saying. Albert Schweitzer, the recipient of the Nobel Peace Prize in 1952, once said, "Success is not the key to happiness. Happiness is the key to success. If you love what you are doing, you will be successful." If a person's life-long pursuit is aimed at **accumulating**

在資本主義社會，擁有大量財富似乎是成功的主要指標。流行文化是如此地推崇富裕者以至於有錢人已經變成新的貴族。然而，如果一個人深入探討成功的元素，他很可能會發現財富幾乎不可能滿足那些元素，這正是我不同意題目敘述的原因。

我確信一個人對他的所作所為是否保持熱誠才是關鍵。我的看法呼應艾伯特・史懷哲的名言。艾伯特・史懷哲是 1952 年的諾貝爾和平獎得主，他曾說「成功不是達到幸福的關鍵。幸福才是達到成功的關鍵。如果你熱愛你做的事，你就會成功」。若一個人終生追求的目標是盡量累積財富，他注定活得像小氣財神。小氣

305

304

話題中搭配名人經歷和電影等，切入主題＋引起考官共鳴
・於寫作話題中納入更生活化表達，不詞窮、漸進式引入主題，毫不費力寫出考官青睞的佳作，巧妙應對多元百變寫作話題，每題大作文均游刃有餘。

雙效強化「寫」＋「說」，一魚兩吃：

‧寫作和口說技能彼此相互影響，寫作能力提升的同時亦修正口說中語法表達錯誤，且口說話題和寫作話題亦有重疊，雙效強化兩個技能，高效攻略「寫」＋「說」。

---

success is Oprah Winfrey, a billionaire and a media **mogul**. In the 1990s, while most talk shows produced **confrontational** content, Winfrey boldly changed the style of her talk show to the one that was based on positive intention. Besides, Winfrey found her gift for communication early, as she started working in a radio station at 16. Knowing one's gift is one of the most **salient** characteristics of successful people. Another celebrity who demonstrates this feature is Ang Lee, two- time winner of the Academy Award for Best Director, who discovered his gift for writing scripts during **adolescence**.

However, the aforementioned traits will not be **actualized** into **attainment** without belief in oneself and making perseverant efforts. Both Winfrey and Lee under went experiences of

312

溫佛瑞大膽地將她的談話性節目的風格改變成以正向意圖為出發點。此外，當溫佛瑞十六歲開始在廣播電台工作時，早就發現她對溝通的才華。瞭解自我的才華是成功人士最顯著的特色之一。另一位展現這項特色的名人是李安，他是兩次奧斯卡金像獎最佳導演獎的得主，李安在青少年時期就發現自己有寫劇本的才華。

然而，如果不相信自己和缺乏堅持不懈的努力，以上所提的特質都不會具體化為成就。溫佛瑞和李安都有不被肯定的經驗，這些經驗原本可能動搖他們發展才華的決心，但

Unit 11　人生觀：取得成功應具備的特質—搭配名人故事：李安與歐普拉‧溫佛瑞

invalidation, which might have **swayed** their determination to develop their talents, yet they believed in themselves despite others' disapproval. Ang Lee has written about his struggle of being a stay-at-home father and having his scripts constantly rejected. Winfrey described how she was **invalidated** because of her gender and ethnic identity. Also, they had **persevered** in making endeavors for decades before acquiring their success. I believe that **endeavor** is the key; without efforts, the other characteristics will hardly impel any achievement.

To sum up, among the four features, continuous endeavors should be the universally acknowledged key feature.

是儘管別人不認同，他們還是相信自己。李安曾經描寫他以往當家庭主夫及劇本不斷被退回掙扎。溫佛瑞曾描述她因性別和種族身份而不被肯定。而且，他們在獲得成功前，堅持不懈地努力，長達數十年。我相信努力是關鍵，沒有努力，其他的特質很難激發任何成就。

總而言之，這四個特質中，持續努力應該是普世公認的關鍵特質。

313

範文內均「粗體字」標示，
迅速掌握 7.5 分以上寫作高分字彙：
· 適時將高分字彙運用在寫作中並拿捏得宜，拉高
字彙使用單項成績，初學乍練即考取寫作 7 以上
的成績，迅速突破 6.5 分寫作魔咒。

lure consumers into spending more, but never feeling satisfied since new products are launched rapidly. Thus, people who seek happiness from **materialism** are trapped in the **vicious** cycle of desiring more and having their desires satisfied only **temporarily**.

Secondly, as most of us belonging to the **bourgeoisie** climb the social ladder, it is difficult to strike a balance between family and work. While we are constantly **swamped** by work demands, we forget to pause and remind ourselves to **appreciate** what we already have. Examples abound that many men already have **affectionate** families, yet they still desire more power or wealth, which is portrayed in the movie, *Click*. The protagonist in *Click* is a **workaholic** who keeps ignoring his family as he strives to meet the demands

快樂的人們會陷於想要更多，而欲望只能暫時被滿足的惡性循環。

第二，當大多數屬於中產階級的我們在社會上力爭上游時，很難在家庭和工作間取得平衡。當我們不斷被工作要求淹沒時，我們會忘記暫停一下並提醒自己體會已經擁有的事物。很多例子顯示許多人已經更多權力或財富，電影《命運好玩》描繪了這現象。《命運好玩》的主角是個工作狂，當他努力要達到老闆的要求及成為公司合夥人的目標時，他一直忽略他的家庭。最終，由於一個神奇遙控器掌控了他的世界，他對人生失去控制，雖然他原本想要用這遙控

Unit 12　人們不滿足於現狀 ─ 搭配電影《命運好玩》（*Click*）

from his boss and his goal to make partner in his company. He ultimately pays the price of losing his family as his life **spiraled** out of control due to a magic remote control that overtakes his universe, though initially he intends to use the remote to fast forward the time to his promotion.

In conclusion, it has become a social norm to be discontent and aspire more, which, when developed to the extreme, might place us in the predicament as symbolized by the **metaphorical** remote in *Click*.

器將時間快轉到他升遷的時刻，他也付出失去家人的代價。

總而言之，不滿足並變筆更多已經變成社會常態，當這現象發展至極端時，可能會讓我們處於像《命運好玩》裡的遙控器隱喻象徵的困境。

Part 1 單句中英互譯　Part 2 段落中譯英　Part 3 精選大作文

318

319

011

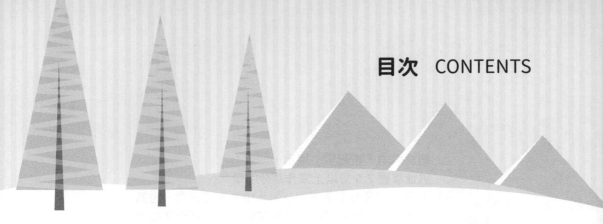

目次 CONTENTS

OR Code 音檔下載

Part 1 單句中英互譯

Part 2　段落中譯英

Part 3 精選大作文

獨家規劃「單句中英互譯」練習，能寫好一個英文句子才具備寫一篇英文作文的基礎，通過百句單句演練後，養成基礎寫作實力和寫出百變句型的能力，自己就能制定計劃強化寫作實力。

PART 1

❶ A contract without formal acceptance is usually not considered to be legally binding to either party.

❷ The renewal of the contract is automatic unless a six-month termination notice is received.

❸ Negotiating an employment contract may sound intimidating, especially for a new graduate.

❹ During mediation last week, the company attempted to settle with the manufacturer but failed.

❺ She interviewed young adults in Tokyo to do an analysis of consumer trends in the fashion market.

❶ 未經正式接納的合約在正常情況下通常不對任何一方有法律約束力。

❷ 除非提前六個月收到合約終止通知，否則合約會自動續約。

❸ （與雇主）談判聘僱契約可能聽起來很恐怖，尤其對職場新鮮人來說。

❹ 在上周的調停中，這家公司曾嘗試與製造商和解，但並沒有成功。

❺ 她訪問東京的年輕人以分析流行服裝市場中的消費者趨勢。

❻ The best-selling smartphone on the market has an attractive design, useful features, and cutting-edge functions.

❼ To attract the attention of younger consumers, the company should have advertised on social media websites rather than the newspaper.

❽ Companies encourage celebrities and athletes to use their products because it will lead to more awareness and increased revenue.

❾ She argued with the manager when she found out that accidental damage was not covered by the basic warranty.

❿ My car has the most reliable warranty of all because it covers damages for three years and includes roadside assistance.

❻ 市場上最熱銷的智慧型手機有迷人的設計、實用的特色與最尖端的功能。

❼ 那間公司本該用社群媒體網站打廣告來吸引年輕消費者，而非報紙。

❽ 各家公司鼓勵明星與運動員使用他們的產品，因為可以提升認知度與增加收益。

❾ 當她發現意外損壞不含在基本保固內時和經理吵了一架。

❿ 我的車的保固最可靠，因為它包含三年的損傷保固與道路救援。

▶▶ UNIT 2 模擬試題（二）

❶ The number of units sent back for replacement was more than we expected, so the product was pulled off the market.

❷ If the item is not repaired by the end of the warranty period, the warranty period will be extended.

❸ The initial step of creating a business plan is writing a summary about your company profile and goals.

❹ She made her business a success through unique marketing strategies that gave her a competitive advantage over other businesses.

❺ Thoroughly research the market and competitors, and you will be able to increase your business success rate.

❶ 送回更換的產品量比我們想像的多，所以產品被下架了。

❷ 如果這個產品在保固期間的尾聲還沒修好的話，保固期限會被延長。

❸ 做營運計畫的第一步就是寫公司概況與目標。

❹ 她事業有成來自於其具備了特殊的行銷策略，這也使她擁有其他企業所沒有的競爭優勢。

❺ 仔細研究市場與競爭對手，你就可以增加你事業的成功率。

6 If you can clearly identify the responsibilities of your management team, your employees will work well together.

7 Attending business conferences is a good way to connect with people who have the same interests.

8 The office is empty because all our employees are preparing to host the international business conference next month.

9 I will submit a proposal describing the purpose and content of my presentation for the conference.

10 Every participant is required to pay the conference registration fee which includes meals and conference materials.

❻ 若你能清楚地辨識你負責團隊的責任，你的員工就能合作無間。

❼ 參加商業會議是個與有相同興趣的人聯繫的好方法。

❽ 全部的員工都在準備下個月我們主辦的國際商務會議，所以辦公室是空的。

❾ 我會繳交計畫書描述我會議報告的目的與內容。

❿ 每位與會者都須繳交報名費，報名費含餐點與會議資料。

▶▶ UNIT 3 模擬試題（三）

❶ Students are often taking free online courses provided by well-known universities to increase their skills and qualifications.

❷ Users can interact and collaborate with people from all over the world through social media tools.

❸ Computer and Internet use are becoming increasingly commonplace not only in schools but also in homes.

❹ Internet connection speed depends on the use and number of users, but eight megabits per second is usually satisfactory.

❺ Organizational office technology helps workers to communicate with clients, manage payment information, and analyze sales data.

❶ 學生經常上名校提供的免費線上課程以增加技能與條件。

❷ 使用者可透過社交媒體與世界各地的人互動與合作。

❸ 使用電腦與網路已不只在學校越來越平常，在家裡也是如此。

❹ 網路連線速度根據使用內容以及使用人數不同，但通常每秒 8MB 就夠了。

❺ 組織辦公科技協助員工與客戶聯繫、管理收付款資訊以及分析銷售資料。

⑥ He has been using his smartphone to make credit card transactions ever since he first started his business.

⑦ Companies regularly upgrade their office technology to increase their productivity and attract future employees.

⑧ Employees who know how to use office technology are usually more accurate than employees who do not.

⑨ It would be wise to follow office procedures whenever customers want to file a complaint.

⑩ New employees should read the company manual and become familiar with the rules before their first day of work.

Part 1 單句中英互譯

Part 2 段落中譯英

Part 3 精選大作文

❻ 他從開始創業之後就一直使用智慧型手機做信用卡付款。

❼ 企業經常更新辦公室科技來增加他們的生產力並吸引未來的員工。

❽ 懂得善用辦公室科技的員工通常會比不懂的員工更精確。

❾ 每當有客戶抱怨的時候，最好遵循辦公室的流程。

❿ 新進員工在開始上班之前應研讀公司手冊並熟悉公司規範。

❶ Everyone needs to know about the emergency exits and safety tools in case a dangerous situation occurs.

❷ Please read the manual carefully because it provides important information about the dress code and holidays.

❸ Security cameras are installed at every entrance and exit to ensure the safety of employees.

❹ A computer, high-speed internet access, and a file cabinet are needed to set up an efficient home office.

❺ She decided to invest her money into starting a small cellphone and laptop repair business at home.

Paper shredders are the quickest way to get rid of private

❶ 每個人都應該要知道緊急出口與急救工具，以防緊急狀況發生。

Please send out the correspondence to our customers to

❷ 請仔細閱讀手冊，因為手冊提供了服裝要求與節日相關的重要資訊。

Correspondences can be used to send a complaint about an employee.

❸ 在每個出入口都裝有監視攝影機來確保員工的安全。

An apology letter was mailed to customers after private

❹ 想設立一個有效率的家庭辦公室，你需要一台電腦、高速網路與檔案櫃。

Writing business letters is important for giving employees

❺ 她決定投入資金在家創立一個小型的手機電腦修護生意。

Part 1 單句中英互譯

Part 2 段落中譯英

Part 3 精選大作文

⑥ Paper shredders are the quickest way to get rid of private documents and protect company information.

⑦ Please send out the correspondence to our customers to inform them about our new policies.

⑧ Correspondences can be used to send a complaint about an employee's actions or company's services.

⑨ An apology letter was mailed to customers after private information was accidentally leaked on May 17th.

⑩ Writing business letters is important for giving employees information about projects and assignments.

❻ 碎紙機是消除機密文件、保護公司資訊的最快方法。

❼ 請將這份信件寄給我們的客人，告知他們新的政策。

❽ 信件能被用來抱怨某個職員的行為或公司的服務。

❾ 在五月十七日個人資訊意外流出後，道歉函便被寄給客戶。

❿ 書寫職場商業信件對給予員工關於專案和任務的相關訊息來說很重要。

▶▶ UNIT 5 模擬試題（五）

❶ Recruiting capable and suitable candidates is critical to the success of an organization.

❷ A recruiter is hired to review resumes, negotiate salaries, and match candidates with appropriate positions.

❸ Companies are always trying to create unique job advertisements to set themselves apart from other companies.

❹ Employers want to hire the most likeable candidate with intelligence, integrity, and leadership skills.

❺ If a student wants to get a job, he or she needs to prepare a resume, write a cover letter, and take employment tests.

❶ 招募有能力又適合的應試者對一個組織的成功與否是個重要的關鍵。

❷ 招募人員被聘來審閱履歷、談判薪資以及將人選媒合至適當的位置。

❸ 公司總是試著創造獨特的求職廣告以和其他公司做出區隔。

❹ 雇主想要聘請有智慧、正直且有領導能力，又最討喜的應徵者。

❺ 若一個學生想找到工作，他（她）必須準備履歷、撰寫應徵函並接受雇用測驗。

❻ In the United States, jobs in leisure, hospitality, health care, social assistance, and finance have been increasing.

❼ During the job application process, applicants must persuade employers to hire them by clearly stating their qualifications and availability.

❽ Employees are searching for companies that encourage diversity and provide career advancement opportunities.

❾ The student prepared for his job interview by recording practice interviews, for he really wanted a job.

❿ Everybody was asked to complete his or her evaluation of the candidates based on skill, character, and professionalism.

❻ 在美國休閒、觀光服務業、醫療保健、社會服務以及財經產業的工作機會一直在增加。

❼ 在工作應徵的過程中，應徵者應清楚闡述他們的條件與可上班時間，以說服雇主聘用他們。

❽ 員工都在尋找鼓勵多元化並提供晉升機會的公司。

❾ 那位學生錄他的面試練習來作應徵工作的準備，因為他真的很想要有工作。

❿ 所有人都被要求根據技能、人格特質與專業來完成他們對候選人的評量。

▶▶ UNIT 6 模擬試題（六）

❶ After employees are hired, each employee needs to receive training in safety, personal growth, and career development.

❷ During the training period, employees are asked to submit several papers on the effective use of technology.

❸ Employers are required to inform employees about customer service skills and workplace safety.

❹ Trainees are highly encouraged to take business writing classes so that they can write as clearly as current employees.

❺ The trainees are meeting upstairs to review communication strategies and organizational policies.

❶ 員工被聘用後，每個人都需要接受安全、個人成長以及事業發展上的訓練。

❷ 在實習的階段，員工會被要求提交好幾份關於有效率使用科技產品的報告。

❸ 雇主有義務告知員工客戶服務技巧與職業安全。

❹ 實習生被積極鼓勵上商業寫作課，書寫內容才能如目前員工一樣清楚。

❺ 實習生要在樓上開會，探討溝通策略與組織政策。

6 Although the salary was not as high, she chose the job with health care and life insurance.

7 If the candidates get hired, the company will offer them a full benefit package in addition to a competitive salary.

8 Before accepting a job offer, prospective employees should consider how much their skills are worth and how much money they want.

9 A few progressive companies allow male employees to take time off of work after the birth or adoption of a child.

10 Employees who have improved their productivity and completed important projects will have a better salary than those who didn't improve.

❻ 雖然薪水相對之下沒有那麼高，但她選了有健保與壽險的工作。

❼ 如果應徵者被聘用了，公司除了與同業相符的薪資外，還會提供完整的福利。

❽ 在接受工作邀約之前，潛在員工應該考慮他們技能的價值以及他們希望的薪資。

❾ 有一些比較先進的公司允許男性員工在孩子出生或是領養孩子之後放假。

❿ 有增進生產力並完成重要專案的員工比起其他沒進步的員工會得到較好的薪水。

▶▶ UNIT 7 模擬試題（七）

❶ If you are interested in signing up for a pension plan, please attend the information session on Thursday.

❷ Employees need to think about which type of pension plan would meet their needs after retirement.

❸ After his presentation, George was immediately promoted because it was clear that he was capable enough to think for himself.

❹ Employees will not be able to receive the employee of the month award unless they excel in sales, customer service, and attendance.

❺ After becoming employee of the month, employers can either get cash rewards or enjoy paid time off.

❶ 如果你想要參加退休金計畫，請參加星期四的説明會。

❷ 員工需要思考哪種退休金計畫可以符合他們退休後的需求。

❸ 完成簡報後，George 馬上被升職，因為很明顯的他懂得獨立思考。

❹ 員工除非在銷售、客戶服務以及出席都表現優異，否則不會得到當月優秀員工獎。

❺ 在成為當月優秀員工後，員工可以得到現金獎勵或是享受帶薪休假。

6 When going shopping, creating a shopping list will help shoppers to stay focused on shopping effectively.

7 It is better to go grocery shopping after you have eaten a big meal, so you don't buy unnecessary items.

8 Either the accountant or the managers have the receipts we need to apply for a tax reduction.

9 Ordering office supplies is a necessary part of every business, and it helps businesses to operate effectively and consistently.

10 When ordering business supplies, the first step is to gather information about the services and product quality of the vendors.

UNIT 6 模擬試題（六）

❻ 去購物時，列出購物清單能讓購物者專注且買起來有效率。

❼ 最好在吃完大餐後才去採買日常用品，避免購入不需要的商品。

❽ 會計或是經理持有我們需要用來申請稅捐扣除額的發票。

❾ 訂購辦公室耗材對每個企業來説都是不可或缺的部分，因為它讓企業更能有效率且一致的運作。

❿ 當訂購商業耗材時，第一步是收集各廠商的服務與產品品質相關資訊。

Before buying an expensive item, buyers should make the make sure they agree with the payment terms.

▶▶▶ UNIT 8 模擬試題（八）

❶ Review this list carefully before you order because it includes important information about the storage and retrieval.

❷ When shipping items, you can ship it overnight, within one to three business days, or within two to eight business days.

❸ Although shipping by air is quicker, shipping by sea is more environmentally friendly because of lower CO_2 emissions.

❹ Wednesdays are our busiest days because we receive shipments hourly from all over the world.

❺ Before buying an expensive item, buyers should check the invoice and make sure they agree with the payment terms.

❶ 訂購之前，仔細審閱這張清單。因為這張清單包含庫存與出貨資訊。

❷ 運送物品時，你可選擇隔夜送達、一到三個工作天送達，或兩到八個工作天送達。

❸ 雖然航空寄件比較快，但船運對環境比較友善，因為二氧化碳排放量較低。

❹ 星期三是我們最忙的一天，因為我們每小時都從世界各地收到貨運。

❺ 在買昂貴的東西之前，買家應該檢查發票，確定同意付款條件。

6 For sellers, invoices are contracts and bills that can be used as a demand for payment until it is paid in full

7 Although sellers see invoices as sales invoices, buyers see them as purchase invoices.

8 Inventory management is required for many locations of a supply network anywhere to proceed with production.

9 An inventory should include a record of everything done prior to sale to be aware of lead time and seasonal demand.

10 Inventory records may give insight into when some items will sell quickly at the highest price.

❻ 對銷售員來說，發票是在費用付清前能用來收款的合約與帳單。

❼ 雖然銷售員視發票為銷售單據，但買家將之視為購買單據。

❽ 存貨管理在任何一個供應鏈中的多個地點都是必要的，如此才能進行製造。

❾ 存貨盤點報表應包含販售前的一切紀錄，以明瞭前置時間與季節需求。

❿ 存貨紀錄可能可以看出哪些時候某些商品可用最高的價錢快速賣出。

▶▶ UNIT 9 模擬試題（九）

❶ Most banks only have a portion of the assets needed to cover their financial obligations.

❷ Banks accept deposits from customers, raise capital from investors, and then provide additional services to customers.

❸ In order to make money, banks tend to lend money at an interest rate higher than their operating and maintenance costs.

❹ Working as an accountant for this firm means you have to spend some time getting used to working remotely.

❺ Bookkeepers may have slightly different tasks from accountants, but bookkeepers are regulated as accountants are.

Part 1 單句中英互譯

Part 2 段落中譯英

Part 3 精選大作文

❶ 大部分的銀行只需資產的一部分來負擔金融債務。

❷ 銀行接受客戶的存款、向投資人募資金，然後提供額外的服務給客戶。

❸ 為了賺錢，銀行傾向以比營運與維修成本還高的利息出借現金。

❹ 在這家事務所當會計表示你必須花時間習慣遠距離工作。

❺ 簿記員的任務可能與會計有些不同，但簿記員受到的規範和會計是一樣的。

⑥ There are some tricks that allow wealthy individuals to pay as little tax as legally possible.

⑦ The guideline states that all investment gains and losses are to be reported to the taxing authority.

⑧ Once registered, you can access your account through the website and invest online.

⑨ An open-end investment company is a company where new shares are created for new investors.

⑩ Before releasing your tax information, you need to sign a written authorization.

❻ 有些技巧讓有錢人能在法律範圍內付越少稅越好。

❼ 規範指出所有的投資獲利與損失都要報告給稅務機關。

❽ 你一旦登記完畢，就可以從網站進入你的帳號，並在線上投資。

❾ 開放型投資公司是創造新股票給新投資者的公司。

❿ 在公開你的稅務資訊前，你應該先簽屬書面授權書。

▶▶ UNIT 10 模擬試題（十）

❶ Our company, as many others, files a tax return with the IRS every fiscal year, declaring our revenue and capital gains.

❷ The business owner has applied for bankruptcy before, so he needs to confirm whether he can file again.

❸ If the firm suffered heavy losses, its balance sheet would not be as strong as last year.

❹ All valuable tangible and intangible assets must be reflected in the financial statement.

❺ Today several leading companies released their financial statement for the fiscal year.

❶ 如同其他很多公司一樣，我們公司每個會計年度都會向 IRS 報稅，申報我們的收入與資本利得。

❷ 業主已申請過破產，需要確認是否可再次申請。

❸ 假如這間公司損失慘重，今年的資產負債表就會不如去年強勢。

❹ 所有有價值的有形與無形資產都應反映在財務報表裡。

❺ 今天數個龍頭公司發布了他們本財政年度的財務報告。

❻ The International Sales Department will take over when the project reaches its third phase.

❼ By this time next week, the new receivable policy will have been implemented.

❽ Part of his job is to ensure all reports detailing the fixed assets registered meet the requirements.

❾ It is the responsibility of the Production Department to fix and manage these fixed assets.

❿ This speaker was able to provide more comprehensive explanations on depreciation than the last.

❻ 待這個計畫進入第三階段時，國際銷售部門便會接手。

❼ 下周的這個時候，新的應收帳款政策已開始執行。

❽ 他工作的一部份便是檢閱所有詳述已登記的固定資產的報告，確保這些報告都符合規定。

❾ 維修與管理這些固定資產是製造部門的責任。

❿ 這位講者比前一位講者更能針對折舊提供完整的解釋。

▶▶▶ UNIT 11 模擬試題（十一）

❶ After hours of negotiation, the board members were still not able to reach a consensus in the meeting.

❷ The board would like to receive updates every six months on the implementation of the plan.

❸ The new chairman has been overly critical of some of the senior members.

❹ After the scandal, the committee calls for ensuring support to those with little power.

❺ Before the scandal was leaked, the committee seemed to have opened a secret investigation.

❶ 經過數個小時的協商，董事們在會議中仍舊無法得到共識。

❷ 董事會希望每六個月可以收到計畫實施的進度報告。

❸ 新的主席一直對部分資深董事過度批評。

❹ 在那件醜聞之後，委員會提倡應確保弱勢族群得到的支持。

❺ 在醜聞流出前，委員會似乎已先開啟秘密調查。

⑥ Since quality control is essential throughout the whole process, all employees should be made aware of the control policy.

⑦ We use three quality control techniques, namely ISO 9000 series, statistical process control, and Six Sigma.

⑧ In accordance with the quality control requirements, all batches have to be tested before being shipped to customers.

⑨ All products received will be inspected on the next day.

⑩ For years, the company has been fully devoted to perfecting its quality assurance procedure.

❻ 既然品質控管對整個程序都很重要，所有的職員都應了解控管的政策。

❼ 我們使用了三種品管手法，即 ISO 9000 系列標準、統計製程管制與六標準差。

❽ 根據品質控制要求，所有貨物出貨給客戶前都必須先驗過。

❾ 所有產品在收到之後，都會在隔天進行檢驗。

❿ 數年間，這家公司全心投入在使其品質保證流程更完善。

▶▶ UNIT 12 模擬試題（十二）

① The division has been focusing on developing software tools for automation systems since 2009.

② Don't forget to conduct market research before you start designing a product.

③ We had the product packaging completely redesigned because it didn't match the company's ethos.

④ We are thinking about performing test marketing before the launch.

⑤ The engineer is asked to create a prototype which can demonstrate these features to customers.

❶ 那個部門從 2009 年開始便致力於研發自動化系統的軟體工具。

❷ 在開始設計產品之前別忘了先進行市場調查。

❸ 我們完全重新設計產品包裝，因為舊包裝並不符合公司精神。

❹ 我們在考慮產品上市前要進行試銷。

❺ 那位工程師被要求做出能展現這些功能給客戶的原型。

⑥ We are renting our property fully furnished so that it would be more marketable and attract a higher rent.

⑦ There are several routes by which you can extend your lease and you should always consult your legal advisor.

⑧ The landlord is demanding that they sign another yearly lease after having been there under two one-year leases.

⑨ The tech company is interested in leasing the office space.

⑩ You should check for damages or scratches when the rental agency hands the car to you.

❻ 我們要以傢俱設備齊全的狀態出租我們的房子，好讓房子更有市場價值、訂的租金可以更高。

❼ 有幾種途徑可以延長租約，而你應該諮詢你的法律顧問。

❽ 房東在他們已經簽過兩次一年的租約後又要求他們再簽一年的租約。

❾ 那間科技公司有興趣租下那個辦公室。

❿ 在租車公司給你車時，你應該要檢查是否有損傷或刮傷。

▶▶ UNIT 13 模擬試題（十三）

❶ She is devoted to trying every restaurant in the Michelin Guide.

❷ When selecting a restaurant, remember that you should be able to enjoy good food without breaking the bank.

❸ While I was walking around the area, I encountered this lovely restaurant.

❶ 4   I had to send my steak back and ask them to cook it more because there is still blood in it.

❺ I heard that caviar tastes very good with white asparagus.

❶ 她全心投入在嘗試米其林指南上的每一家餐廳。

❷ 在選擇餐廳時，記得你並不需要花大把鈔票也可以享受美食。

❸ 我在那附近逛的時候，看見一家很可愛的餐廳。

❹ 我必須退回我的牛排請他們煎久一點，因為裡面還有血色。

❺ 我聽說魚子醬與白蘆筍配起來很美味。

❻ He has been looking for red wine and some fresh fruit to make sangria for half an hour.

❼ Since the manager is paying, you can order any food on the menu.

❽ Not until we almost finished discussing all matters did we receive our lunch.

❾ The restaurant that offers the best food and each order is accompanied by its signature chocolate biscuit.

❿ Contact the person if you are interested in becoming a private chef.

❻ 他找了紅酒與一些新鮮水果要做桑格力亞酒已經找了半小時了。

❼ 因為是經理付錢，你可以點菜單上任何一種食物。

❽ 直到我們快結束討論所有議題，我們才收到午餐。

❾ 那家餐廳的食物非常棒，且每次訂餐都附餐廳最有名的巧克力餅乾。

❿ 如果你有興趣當私人廚師，聯絡那個人。

▶▶ UNIT 14 模擬試題（十四）

❶ She used to be the line chef in that famous restaurant, but now she owns three restaurants.

❷ To become a chef, you don't have to go to a culinary school first if you're willing to work your way up from the bottom.

❸ At this time next week, we will be doing our first catering order for 300 people.

❹ She was forced to host the party by herself since everyone in the office was busy with other projects.

❺ To commit to sustainability, we are asking everyone attending the wine tasting event to bring your own glass.

① 她原本是那家名餐廳的二廚，但現在擁有三間餐廳。

② 要成為廚師，如果你願意從底層做起，你不一定要先唸廚藝學校。

③ 下禮拜的這個時間，我們將在為三百人進行我們的第一次外燴訂單。

④ 因為辦公室的人都在忙其他案子，她被迫自己主持派對。

⑤ 為致力於永續發展，我們請求參加品酒活動的各位攜帶自己的酒杯。

⑥ Wake up early should you want to have the best attractions all to yourself.

⑦ The travel agency suggested that he check with the hotel to find out what to see in Nairobi.

⑧ Interacting with locals allows you to gain a deeper understanding of a culture. Besides, it can also give you more memorable experiences.

⑨ Pearson International Airport has tightened their security procedures since the attack that killed 36 people.

⑩ A ticket to Melbourne now costs only around USD180 if you're willing to fly red-eye.

❻ 如果你想要獨自享受所有美好的觀光景點，你應該早起。

❼ 旅行社建議他詢問飯店，了解奈洛比可以參觀的景點。

❽ 除了能更深入了解一個文化之外，與當地人互動可以給你更難忘的經驗。

❾ 皮爾森國際機場自從一場攻擊造成 36 人死亡後，便加強了安檢程序。

❿ 現在一張去墨爾本的機票只要美金 180 元，如果你願意飛紅眼航班的話。

Part 1 單句中英互譯

Part 2 段落中譯英

Part 3 精選大作文

UNIT 15 模擬試題（十五）

❶ Most fliers find it annoying to wait for hours in lengthy security lines and secretly hope to avoid the wait.

❷ These luxury trains are too expensive for locals and are meant for international travelers.

❸ Dining on the dinner train is such a special experience that I cannot recommend it enough.

❹ There are two types of seats on the train. One is the cheaper hard seat and the other is the more expensive soft seat.

❺ When I chose the hotel, I not only looked at rates but also paid attention to location.

❶ 大部分的旅客都討厭在冗長的安檢隊伍中等上好幾個小時，並偷偷地希望可以避開。

❷ 這些豪華火車對當地人來說太貴，原本就是設計給國際旅客的。

❸ 在火車上用餐的經驗實在太特別，我讚不絕口。

❹ 這火車有兩種座位，一種是較便宜的硬式座位，另一種是較貴的軟式座位。

❺ 我選這家飯店時，不只看了費率，還注意了地點。

⑥ Booking hotels is one of the most important but difficult decisions one has to make when organizing trips.

⑦ When you arrive at the hotel, you should familiarize yourself with your hotel's emergency plan.

⑧ It is high rental rates that are driving all the customers to other agencies.

⑨ Fast Care Hire is said to offer the best deals and services, which is why people always go there when they need to rent a car.

⑩ As the busy summer car-rental season is approaching, prices are climbing.

❻ 訂飯店是在安排旅遊時最重要但最困難的決定之一。

❼ 當你抵達飯店的時候，你應該先熟悉飯店的緊急應變計畫。

❽ 正是高額的租車費把客戶都趕到其他租車公司去了。

❾ 據說 Fast Care Hire 提供的價格與服務是最好的，也因此大家如果需要租車都去那。

❿ 隨著夏天的租車季節接近，價錢也在攀升中。

▶▶▶ UNIT 16 模擬試題（十六）

❶ The girl doesn't like sci-fi movies. Can you suggest one of a different genre?

❷ The director used fewer sound effects in her latest movie because she wanted the viewers to focus on the performance of the characters.

❸ As soon as he gets the tickets and snacks, he will enter the auditorium to get better seats.

❹ I go to the theater very often despite having to pay quite a lot for a show.

❺ Watching an opera in the Sydney Opera House is what I want to do when I arrive in Sydney.

Part 1 單句中英互譯

Part 2 段落中譯英

Part 3 精選大作文

❶ 那個女孩並不喜歡科幻片，你可不可以建議另一種類型的電影。

❷ 導演在她最新的電影裡使用較少的聲效，因為她希望觀眾能專注在角色的演出上。

❸ 一買到票跟零食，他就會進場找好位置。

❹ 儘管一場秀不便宜，我還是常常上劇場。

❺ 在雪梨歌劇院裡看一齣歌劇是我一到雪梨就想做的事。

6 I can't remember which Broadway musical we watched during our last trip to New York.

7 He will go to the Woodstock Festival in New York unless the flight is canceled.

8 The singer will not be releasing a new album until the contract dispute with the record label is resolved.

9 I always can't help wanting to listen to Sam Smith on a rainy day.

10 The museum is facing closure because of the recession and budget cuts and many are preparing to protest.

Part 1 單句中英互譯

Part 2 段落中譯英

Part 3 精選大作文

❻ 我想不起來我們上一次到紐約旅行時看的百老匯音樂劇是哪一部。

❼ 除非班機被取消，否則他會去紐約的胡士托音樂節。

❽ 那個歌手在跟唱片公司的合約糾紛解決之前不會出新專輯。

❾ 下雨時我總是忍不住想聽 Sam Smith 的歌。

❿ 因為經濟不景氣與預算縮減，博物館將關閉，而許多人正準備抗爭。

UNIT 17 模擬試題（十七）

1 The museum will increase guards and surveillance cameras for fear of being burglarized again.

2 As the exhibitions are periodically rearranged, I recommend visiting the museum whenever you feel like it.

3 According to the news report, the body was found lying in the middle of the street with gunshot wounds.

4 Many people feel that the news media are devoting much less time to serious news coverage.

5 The president-elect spoke about his vision for the country in his first interview with The Guardian.

Part 1 單句中英互譯

Part 2 段落中譯英

Part 3 精選大作文

❶ 博物館將會增加警衛與監視器，以免再次遭偷竊。

❷ 因為展出品會定期重新安排，我建議想去的時候就可以再去參觀。

❸ 根據新聞報導，屍體發現時倒在路中央，身上有槍傷。

❹ 許多人覺得新聞媒體報導嚴肅的新聞的時間減少很多。

❺ 總統當選人在他與衛報的第一次訪問中談及了他對國家的願景。

❻ With the help of the latest technology, your doctor can better diagnose your condition.

❼ When you've come down with a cold, there is actually no better cure than rest and fluids.

❽ Emergency rooms do not refuse care to people who need it, nor do they provide the service for free.

❾ Many people in remote areas cannot afford basic needs, let alone visit the dentist for regular dental care.

❿ Most people prefer using ceramic dental crowns to using gold crowns for dental restoration because the former ones look more natural.

Part 1 單句中英互譯

Part 2 段落中譯英

Part 3 精選大作文

❻ 有了最新科技的幫助，你的醫生更能準確的診斷你的狀況。

❼ 感冒的時候，最好的治療其實就是休息和補充水分。

❽ 急診室不會拒絕有治療需要的人，但他們也不會免費提供服務。

❾ 很多在偏遠地區的人無法負擔基本需求，更不用說找牙醫做定期護理。

❿ 大部分人的補牙偏愛使用陶瓷，而不是金，因為前者看起來比較自然。

▶▶ UNIT 18 模擬試題（十八）

1 There are two ways to treat gum diseases, receiving dental treatment and practicing good oral hygiene, and the latter is more important.

2 If you have health insurance, all you need to do is show your insurance card when you go to the doctor.

3 The healthcare system in Taiwan promises that the rich as well as the poor enjoy equal access to healthcare.

4 I'm not going to take the employer-sponsored plan; instead, I'll look for my own health plan.

5 The study showed that patients at the worst hospitals were three times more likely to die than patients at the best hospitals.

❶ 治療牙周病有兩種方法：口腔治療與良好的口腔衛生習慣，而後者更加重要。

❷ 如果你有健保的話，你只需要在看醫生的時候出示你的健保卡即可。

❸ 台灣的健保系統承諾富者與窮者都能平等享有健保。

❹ 我不會參加雇主提供的健保，而是自己找健保計畫。

❺ 研究顯示在最差醫院的病人的死亡機率比在最好醫院的病人的死亡機率高出三倍。

❻ The state-of-the-art hospital in a remote area in India is in fact made of bamboo.

❼ The doctor took a full medical history and performed a detailed examination to find out the real cause of her abdominal pain.

❽ Sometimes the information about a medicine given by the doctor is different from that given by the pharmacist.

❾ When it comes to medication, following directions carefully is most important.

❿ In recent years, several cases of counterfeit drugs have been reported in both developed and developing countries.

❻ 那家在印度偏遠地區，擁有最先進技術的醫院其實是以竹子蓋成的。

❼ 醫生詢問完整的病史並進行詳細的檢查，以找出她腹部疼痛的真正原因。

❽ 有時關於某種藥物的資訊，醫生說得和藥師說得不一樣。

❾ 當說到藥物時，小心遵循說明是最重要的。

❿ 近年來，好幾起假藥事件在已開發和開發中國家都被報導。

❶ Please be aware that all personal correspondence sent from the office computers is subject to review by the management staff.

❷ Those who worked overtime on the weekend to finish the project were given Monday morning off as compensation.

❸ A monthly newsletter highlighting the achievements of the company will especially be sent out to keep the newcomers better informed as well as positive on duty.

❹ Though the company considers the orientation the most efficient method in adjusting rookies to our firm in the very short time, many people find the intensive training schedule rather exhausting.

❺ After all applications are received, the city council will hold a meeting to choose new marketing contractors for the new outlet plaza.

❶ 請注意所有從辦公室電腦所寄出的個人書信皆需受管理階層的審查。

❷ 那些週末超時工作以完成計畫的員工，將給予星期一上午的補休。

❸ 強調公司成就的每月通訊將會特別發送給那些新進人員，讓他們持續被妥善告知，並在工作時保持正面態度。

❹ 雖然公司認為，新生員工訓練是在很短的時間調整新秀、讓他們適應我們公司最有效的方法，但很多人發現，密集的訓練日程是相當累人的。

❺ 在收到所有的申請文件之後，市議會將召開會議，為新的購物廣場選擇新的行銷承包商。

⑥ Concern about the future of many marine animals has led to a rapid reduction in trading of marine products recently, especially those made from international conserved ones.

⑦ The sheer variety of products that we offer for sale are distinctively unmatched by any of our competitors.

⑧ All production is halted, and until the company's profits get improved by 5%, neither side seems prepared to negotiate.

⑨ Delegating easier purchasing projects to inexperienced workers while leaving challenging ones with veterans is suggesting the office operate more efficiently.

⑩ All shipment and packaging waste is under the request of being disposed of, and collected in the agreed receptacles near the rear entrance of the building.

❻ 最近對於許多海洋動物未來的擔憂，導致海洋產品交易迅速減少，特別是那些來自國際保護物種的產品。

❼ 我們的銷售產品多元，對我們的任何競爭對手而言，非常明顯地是無法比擬。

❽ 所有的生產停止，且在公司利潤提升至 5％前，雙方似乎還未能準備好進行協商。

❾ 委派容易採購項目給沒有經驗的工人，然而留給那些具有挑戰性的項目給老手，是希望（建議）辦公室能更有效地運作。

❿ 依要求，所有廢棄物的裝運應集中在集收地做處理。該集收地靠近大樓後方入口處，是經同意而選出的地方。

❶ Due to heavy snow in southern England, many flights from Heathrow Airport have been delayed for up to seven hours.

❷ During the expansion of Hong Kong International Airport, some flights will be relocated to Macau.

❸ Purchasers would find details of our terms in the price list printed on the inside front cover of the catalogue.

❹ Many companies are still reluctant to make major capital investments out of uncertainty over whether the recovery will continue.

❺ This way, your monthly savings deposit takes a small contribution from every paycheck automatically, and you will be surprised how quickly this simple trick can make your savings add up.

❶ 由於英國南部劇烈的降雪，許多從希斯洛機場的航班延誤七小時以上。

❷ 在香港國際機場擴建期間，一些航班將會被重新安置到澳門。

❸ 買家會在產品目錄封面內頁的價格表上，找到我們所印的產品規範。

❹ 在復甦能否持續的不確定中，許多公司仍不願意作出重大資本投資。

❺ 這樣一來，你每月的儲蓄存款會自動從每個月的薪水扣除，而且你會驚奇地發現，這個簡單的技巧可迅速地讓您的儲蓄增加。

⑥ A copy of our prospectus containing particulars of our policies for householders is enclosed.

⑦ Consequently, we are prepared to offer you a total of £4,800 in full compensation under your policy.

⑧ Due to technical problems, our website and mailbox for submission are convinced to be inaccessible for an indeterminate delay.

⑨ In order to finish the file attachment process, a click on the attach button is considered to be a must.

⑩ The newly elected administration has launched an aggressive strategy for federal counterterrorism in hopes of solidifying national security.

❻ 附件是我們計畫書的副本，上有包含我們房屋所有人的保單詳情。

❼ 因此，我們準備為您提供，在您的保單下，共計 4,800 英鎊的全額賠償。

❽ 由於技術問題，我們的網站和交付的郵件信箱因為不明原因的延遲，確定是無法進入的。

❾ 為了完成文件附加的過程，對附件按鈕點擊被認為是必須的。

❿ 新上任的內閣已經推動積極的國家反恐策略，為的是希望鞏固國家安全。

Part 1 單句中英互譯

Part 2 段落中譯英

Part 3 精選大作文

❶ The research findings about hypnosis healing remain inconclusive and controversial; therefore, the curing method still has a long way to go.

❷ Animal rights groups claimed to take more drastic measures unless the cosmetic manufactures stopped inhumane animal tests.

❸ The Internet addiction among adolescents brought about serious academic and personality problems and has gradually aroused social attention.

❹ Thanks to the decreased costs of 3D printers, the technology of the three-dimensional printing has recently gained popularity among different fields of industry.

❺ The financial institution posted an advertisement to offer jobs for business school graduates with innovative consciousness and abilities.

❶ 有關於催眠治療的研究發現依舊是未定且有爭議的；因此，這種治療方式仍有待努力。

❷ 動物權益團體宣稱，除非化妝品製造廠商停止不人道的動物實驗，否則將採取更激烈的手段。

❸ 青少年的網路成癮導致嚴重的課業及人格問題，並且逐漸地引發社會關切。

❹ 幸虧有 3D 立體印刷機的降價，3D 立體印刷科技近日在各個不同產業領域受到歡迎。

❺ 這家金融機構刊登職缺廣告來徵求具創新意識及能力的商學院畢業生。

⑥ Young generations should be taught from their early childhood to practice the 3R Principles — Reduce, Reuse, and Recycle to protect and sustain the earth.

⑦ Mr. Banks is a lawyer specialized in criminal law and is dedicated to defending against criminal charges.

⑧ The dazzling northern lights, also called "the aurora borealis," display one of nature's greatest spectacles, and are unique to only certain regions in Canada, Scotland, Norway, and Sweden.

⑨ The refined merchandise exhibited in the Trade Fair last month was manufactured by Morrison Company and has received great numbers of orders since then.

⑩ The rich and renowned CEO remained modest and was enthusiastic about charitable affairs by donating millions of dollars each year.

❻ 年輕世代應從小被教導力行 3R 原則 ── 減量、重複使用，以及回收，以保護並延續地球。

❼ 班克斯先生是一名專精於刑事訴訟法的律師，並致力於刑事訴訟的辯護。

❽ 炫目的極北之光，又稱為「北極光」，展現大自然絕佳的奇觀之一，並且是加拿大、蘇格蘭、挪威，及瑞典特定地區獨具的景觀。

❾ 上個月在貿易展展示的優質商品是由莫里森公司所製造的，並從那時起接獲大量的訂單。

❿ 這位富有且著名的執行長依舊保持謙遜的態度，並且熱心於每年捐贈數百萬元贊助慈善事業。

▶▶ UNIT 22 模擬試題（二十二）

❶ When Ms. Huang found that the security system was out of order, she called the repairman in to look at it right away.

❷ No sooner had he arrived at his home than he was called back to the office to deal with a matter of urgency.

❸ Starting from next week, headquarters will have entrance permits issued for the use of recruiting employees in the fair.

❹ Many job opportunities made recent graduates from the community college's business program appreciated, for the job fair held by the city government.

❺ The mental reinforcements in ensuring product validity will minimize damage throughout the upcoming price-cutting competition.

❶ 當黃小姐發現負責安全的系統故障時，她立即打電話請維修人員過來檢修。

❷ 他一到家就被公司用電話召回處理這緊急事件。

❸ 從下週起，總部會發出進出許可證，給在商展招募員工的職員所使用。

❹ 近來諸多的工作機會，讓社區學院商業計劃畢業的應屆畢業生相當感謝市政府所舉辦的就業博覽會。

❺ 在心理上強化保證產品的正當性，會在整個即將到來的削價競爭中將損害降到最低。

⑥ Although the output situation seems poor at the moment, we will anticipate a swift improvement once the downturn is over.

⑦ Foreign businessmen often express unexpected amazement at how far our manufacturer can achieve what they originally think impossible.

⑧ In spite of consumer objection, Infocus will spend considerable time expanding the potential benefits of building cell phone plants.

⑨ The problems with the just-in-time supply chain were solved following negotiations with the lead suppliers.

⑩ The man talking on the phone about the lack of compensation after the accident at the oil refinery is getting increasingly angry.

❻ 雖然生產的情況目前看來不佳，當衰退一旦結束，我們預計產量會有快速的進展。

❼ 外國商人對於我們的製造廠商的表現驚訝，因為製造廠商達成了他們原本認為不可能的事情。

❽ 儘管消費者的反對，Infocus 還是會花費相當長的時間，擴大建設手機工廠的潛在好處。

❾ 與即時供應連鎖商的問題被解決，接著與重要的供應商協商。

❿ 在電話上談論有關於在油品精煉廠發生意外之後賠償金不足的男人，愈講愈生氣。

UNIT 23 模擬試題（二十三）

❶ After the accident, all electrical equipment must be checked before any further use.

❷ We understand that you are arranging for immediate delivery from stock, and we look forward to hearing from you soon.

❸ The controversial law regarding team share buying restrictions continues to be protested across the country by various local community retailers.

❹ We highly recommend this book with detailed description of mysterious creatures in ancient fables, and with insight into the possible origins of them.

❺ Our newly-established online stationery shop is committed to providing students and business people with a wide variety of high-quality stationery items as well as PC products and other services.

❶ 意外事件之後，所有用電的設備必須在進一步使用之前檢查。

❷ 我們了解您正在從存貨中安排現貨，以便立即發貨，而我們也期待著能從您那裡儘快得到消息。

❸ 關於球隊股份購買限制的法律引起極大的爭議，抗議聲浪不斷，遍及全國各零售單。

❹ 我們強烈推薦這本書，裡面詳細介紹遠古神話中的神秘生物、並以精闢的見解剖析他們的可能來源。

❺ 我們新成立的網路文具店致力為學生和商務人士服務，提供各種高品質的文具、電腦產品與其他服務。

⑥ When replying to customers' enquiries, be sure you have answered every query in the exhibition.

⑦ The most attractive yet dangerous aspect of the credit system is that you can buy things even if, at the moment, you do not have enough money.

⑧ I am writing in reference to an overdue payment for invoice #5542-87, which is now in excess of three months overdue.

⑨ As you propose to ship regularly, we can offer you a rate of 2.48% benefit interest -- for a total cover of £60,000.

⑩ In particular we wish to know whether you can give a special rate in return for the promise of regular monthly shipments.

❻ 在回答客戶的詢問時，請確保您已經回答了展場的每個詢問。

❼ 信用體系最吸引人，但也是最危險的地方在於，就算那一刻你沒有足夠的錢，你還是可以買東西。

❽ 這封信是要告知您，其中提到的逾期付款發票 # 5542-87，目前逾期超過三個月。

❾ 就你提出定期出貨的建議，我們可提供您總計 60,000 英鎊的保障與$ 2.48%的利率優惠。

❿ 我們特別想知道，你是否可因每月定期運送貨物的承諾，給一個優惠的價格當作回饋。

▶▶ UNIT 24 模擬試題（二十四）

1 It is our pleasure to announce that a new campus e-mail program was created recently, and its headquarters was located in the main building.

2 Keeping up with current innovations and new, emerging services in information technology at the same time seems to be a nearly impossible task to get acquainted with.

3 It is estimated that producing books in hard copy format may bring several million tons of harmful CO_2 into the atmosphere, so E-books are definitely here to stay.

4 According to neuroscientists, approximately 20 percent of short-term memory can be improved by regular physical exercise, especially to the elderly.

5 With versatile pop music superstars creating extraordinary performances, Korean pop music trend has prevailed worldwide.

❶ 我們很榮幸地宣布，新校區的電子郵件程式最近被創立，而它的總部是設在主要大樓。

❷ 要同時熟悉、跟上當前的創新與新興的資科服務，這似乎是一個幾近於不可能達成的任務。

❸ 據估計，製造硬皮書籍可能將數百萬公噸有害的二氧化碳氣體帶入大氣層，所以電子書當然應該普遍推廣。

❹ 根據神經科學家的説法，將近百分之二十短暫的記憶可以經由規律的體能運動得到改善，尤其是對老年人而言。

❺ 有著多才多藝流行音樂超級巨星創造傑出的表演，韓國流行音樂的潮流遍及全世界。

6 Music, with its functions of offering soothing feelings and full relaxation, remains a universal language for all times.

7 Some extreme-sports enthusiasts are capable of achieving difficult and challenging extreme tasks with incredible perfection.

8 Due to wide variations of public opinion, the political figure caught in a dilemma had a hard time getting away from the scandal.

9 The company has recently renewed the computer software, and is working on tests to make sure the new system will be compatible with the existing apparatus.

10 Martin has lived in comfort and luxury ever since he made successful financial investments and piled up a considerable fortune.

❻ 音樂，具有提供舒緩情緒及全面放鬆的功用，一直以來是一個世界性的語言。

❼ 有些極限運動的愛好者有能力以令人難以置信的完美方式達成艱困且具挑戰性的極限任務。

❽ 由於輿論的眾說紛紜，這位深陷進退兩難困境的政治人物很難從醜聞中脫身。

❾ 這家公司最近更新了電腦軟體，並正在測試以確保新的系統與現有的裝置相容。

❿ 馬汀自從金融投資成功且積聚可觀的財富後，一直過著舒適奢華的生活。

❶ I have talked with him about being late for the office twice already, but it hasn't made much of an impression on him.

❷ Nitche Stationery sells a variety of office supplies, and many other   office appliances for nearly a decade, and has been very satisfied with our quality.

❸ Many workers were left unemployed when the company's production facility was shut down due to budget shortfalls.

❹ The Avery Career Center offers advice and assistance to get staff acquired in non-technical professions to further ensure their job positions.

❺ I am writing to inform you that the expired date of your insurance in this product warranty will be further extended as of June 15th for one more year via our promotion campaign.

❶ 我已經跟他提及他 2 次上班遲到的事情，但這對他好像沒啥印象。

❷ 尼采文具這公司販售各種辦公室用品，還有許多其他的辦公室器具將近 10 年的時間，一直以來也十分滿意我們的品質。

❸ 由於預算短缺，該公司的生產設施被迫關閉，留下許多工人失業。

❹ Avery 就業指導中心提供諮詢和協助，讓員工學會非技術的專業，以進一步確保他們的工作職位。

❺ 這封信是為了告訴你，透過我們產品的促銷，您這個產品保固的保險到期日將進一步於 6 月 15 日起被延長一年。

6 We are presenting several interesting variations on the original business model to you, which we have experienced for a long time.

7 Stunned by the impressive performance of the production yield these years, the magazine critic was at a loss for words when he sat down to write a review of the firm.

8 Setting up plants in the commercial districts brings even more profits than in the industrial ones because there is always more consumption in the former ones.

9 With so much shipment company information on the Internet, it is difficult to urge users to notice your website, place orders, or even confirm delivery orders precisely.

10 An outsider cannot but struggle to understand the complexity of the development concerning the automated transportation process as it has evolved today.

❻ 我們將呈現給你一些、針對原有商業模式的有趣變化，而這已經實驗了一段時間。

❼ 當雜誌評論家坐下來寫這間公司的評論時，對其這些年令人印象深刻的生產良率訝異到說不出話來。

❽ 在商業區設廠，比在工業區帶來了更多的利潤，因為在前者的消費量總是較多。

❾ 由於網路到處都是貨運公司的資訊，因此很難督促使用者留意你的網站、下訂單，甚至確認訂貨訂單。

❿ 局外人不得不努力去理解自動運輸過程演變至今的複雜發展。

❶ Could you please send me details of the refrigerators advertised in yesterday's 'Evening Post'?

❷ Visitors in the stadium are quite impressed by our Model Info 2, the newest solar battery.

❸ I appreciate a letter of apology from your department as soon as you have verified these errors made by your clients' account management.

❹ Would you please arrange for $3,000, which is to be transferred from our No. 2 account to their account with Denmark Banks, Leadshell Street, London, on the 1st of every month, beginning 1st May this year?

❺ The personal medical insurance will be effective on our receiving the enclosed proposal form which is completed by you.

Part 1 單句中英互譯

Part 2 段落中譯英

Part 3 精選大作文

❶ 請你能不能寄給我昨天在「晚間郵報」廣告的冰箱細節？

❷ 展場的參訪者對我們的最新的太陽能電池—信息 2 號機型印象深刻。

❸ 您於確認管理客戶帳戶時所犯得錯誤後，便立即自您部門發出了道歉信函，對此我很感激。

❹ 可否請您安排，從今年五月起，每個月的 1 號從我們的 2 號帳戶轉移 3000 美元到他們在倫敦 Leadshell 街丹麥銀行的帳戶？

❺ 當我們一收到你所完成的附件申請表，個人醫療保險將生效。

6 Please send me particulars of your terms and conditions for the policy and a proposal form if required.

7 Doctors believe that the calories you consume could affect many aspects of your health.

8 A fully functional version of the program is made to download the exe files at no cost from the Internet for a 30 day evaluation.

9 Aside from the unbearably high temperatures, global warming is also to blame for the power to go out.

10 Irene had better watch out for those of her gossip friends who may once in a while spread rumors about her.

❻ 如果需要的話，請給我你的保單條款、條件與申請表格的詳情。

❼ 醫生們相信你吃進的熱量可能會影響到健康許多面向。

❽ 該計劃的全功能版本需從網路免費下載 exe 文件，並有 30 天的免費評估時間。

❾ 除了難耐的高溫之外，全球暖化也導致能源的流失。

❿ 艾琳最好要小心她那群偶爾會散播有關於她謠言的八卦朋友。

▶▶ UNIT 27 模擬試題（二十七）

❶ At the present time, scientists spare no efforts to find resources of the alternative energy to substitute for the fossil fuels consumed by industry.

❷ After most of its safety inspections failed to meet the standards, the mall was seriously penalized, and had to make immediate improvement.

❸ Compared with others, people tortured by depression relatively need more care and attention, for they don't easily reveal their emotional problems.

❹ To keep healthy, one should be careful not to consume too much the food that contains additives, such as preservatives, coloring, or artificial flavorings.

❺ The manager informed the factory that they might decrease or even cancel the original orders if the goods shipped in continued to be in poor quality.

❶ 目前來說，科學家們不遺餘力地尋找替代能源的資源來取代工業所消耗的石化燃料。

❷ 在大部分的安全檢驗無法符合標準之後，這個大賣場被嚴厲地處罰，並且必須做立即的改善。

❸ 和一般人比較起來，為憂鬱症所苦的人相對地需要更多的關心和注意，因為他們不輕易地透露他們的情緒問題。

❹ 為了維持健康，人們應該小心不要吃太多含有添加物的食物，例如：防腐劑、色素，或者人工調味料。

❺ 經理通知工廠，假使進貨的商品仍舊品質不良的話，他們會減少或甚至取消原有的訂單。

6 To make both ends meet, Roy had no choice but to take several part-time jobs to generate additional income.

7 The magician's marvelous performances attracted full attention of the audience and won him long and loud applause.

8 People who suffer from a migraine headache can relieve the pain effectively by all forms of relaxation, a lot of water-drinking, or keeping away from noises and bright lights.

9 Mr. Cosby had a serious cold and coughed a lot; thus, he could hardly swallow anything because of the painful throat.

10 The movie adapted from a novel was disappointing to the moviegoers because they could hardly find any consistency between the two.

❻ 為了收支均衡，羅伊不得不兼職數份兼差的工作來賺取額外的
收入。

❼ 魔術師奇妙的表演吸引全場觀眾的目光，並且為自己贏得許久
響亮的喝采聲。

❽ 罹患偏頭痛的人可以藉由各種放鬆的方式，喝大量的水，或遠
離噪音及亮光來有效地紓緩疼痛。

❾ 寇斯比先生由於嚴重的感冒加上咳嗽咳得厲害，以致於喉嚨疼
痛而無法吞嚥任何東西。

❿ 這部由小說改編的電影讓電影觀賞者感到失望，因為他們幾乎
找不出兩者間情節相符之處。

▶▶ UNIT 28 模擬試題（二十八）

1 Best Automobile procured 11 million dollars from the investor last week, making it competitive enough to enter the global market.

2 Best Design hit the headlines with its innovative kitchen wares that can greatly reduce the preparation time for millions of housewives.

3 A piece of software equipment priced at US 500 dollars is considered expensive in the eyes of the dilettante.

4 According to the rituals, rookie pilots are asked to assemble at the canteen before every dinner.

5 Best Furniture has surpassed its rival by launching the unprecedented furnishings that exceed consumers' expectations.

❶ 倍斯特汽車於上週從投資者那裡獲得 1 千 1 百萬元的資金，使其足以具備有進入全球市場的競爭力。

❷ 倍斯特設計公司以其創新的廚具組上了新聞頭條，將替數百萬的家庭主婦大幅地縮短準備時間。

❸ 在業餘者的眼中，一件定價在 500 美元的軟體設備被視為是昂貴的。

❹ 根據老規矩，菜鳥機師被要求要在每次晚餐期間於餐廳內集合。

❺ 藉由推出超越消費者期盼史無前例的傢俱，倍斯特傢俱行已經超越其競爭對手。

⑥ Mass production of milk is worthy of praises, but not during the time when the virus is devastating the globe.

⑦ Although the economy hits us all, Best Watch, a subsidiary of the Fashion Watch, has handed in impressive yields, contrary to what the sources said.

⑧ Analysts are predicting that Best Automobile won't be the beneficiary after the huge merger because there seems to be lots of unresolved issues in the company.

⑨ Unscrupulous vendors had already stockpiled millions of clinical masks before the virus began to ravage people's lives.

⑩ Further down the supply chain, Best Drinks is backed up by ingredient suppliers that help it to produce the best milk tea in town.

6 牛奶的大量生產是值得稱讚的，但在病毒肆虐全球的期間卻恰好相反。

7 儘管我們都受到經濟衝擊，倍斯特手錶，一間時尚手錶的子公司，已繳出了令人欽佩的利潤，這不同於其他消息所述。

8 分析師預測倍斯特汽車不會是巨大合併後的受益者，因為公司似乎仍存在著許多未解的議題。

9 在病毒開始摧毀人命之前，無恥的攤商已經囤積了百萬片的醫療用口罩。

10 在供應鏈之下，倍斯特飲料有著原料供應商的支持，幫助其生產小鎮上的最佳牛乳。

▶▶ UNIT 29 模擬試題（二十九）

❶ Due to the economic downturn, executives in the conference have decided to cut ad expenditures so that the cash flow for the next few months won't be an issue.

❷ Both insufficient tourists visiting in the areas and a significant change in consumer shopping habits have contributed to the significant drop in retailers' revenues.

❸ To encourage the use of the reusable shopping bag, several department stores are rewarding consumers using it during the festival with an additional 10% discount.

❹ For the sake of the incident in the news, store workers are now pretty vigilant about the intruders, especially during the night shift.

❺ To distract the attention of the lion, the circus performer uses the lingering scent of its favorite dishes.

❶ 由於經濟衰退，會議室中的高階主管已經決定要刪減廣告支出，這樣一來接下來幾個月的現金流就不會是個問題。

❷ 參訪此地的觀光客數的不足和消費購物習慣的顯著改變已經導致了零售商總收入的明顯下降。

❸ 為了鼓勵使用可重複性利用的購物袋，幾間百貨公司獎勵在節慶期間使用的消費者享有額外 **10%**的折扣。

❹ 由於新聞事件的緣故，店裡的工人現在對於闖入者相當機警，尤其是在夜間值班期間。

❺ 為了分散獅子的注意力，馬戲團的表演者使用了牠最喜愛餐點的氣味。

❻ Studying marine mammals is harder in good weather conditions, so the professor wants the students to cherish the moment.

❼ The insurance company will not compensate the money to those who self-injury themselves.

❽ In the kindergarten, teachers often underestimate children's curiosity to explore new things in a new environment.

❾ One of the most exhilarating things in the office is the birthday present prepared by the CEO.

❿ For customers who had previously been turned down before can now receive the monetary compensations.

❻ 在天氣良好的時候要研究海洋哺乳類動物都有些難了，所以教授想要學生珍惜這個時刻。

❼ 這間保險公司不會補償那些自我傷害的人金錢。

❽ 在幼稚園裡，老師通常低估了小孩在一個新環境會去探索新事物的好奇心。

❾ 在辦公室內，其中最令人感到振奮的事情是由執行長所準備的生日禮物。

❿ 對於先前受到拒絕的顧客現在可以收到金錢的補償了。

❶ In 2010, Best Cellphone began to lose its advantage to the rival company and the stock price dropped as well.

❷ Unable to find outside investors to finance, Best Clothing has to make the cut of at least 10,000 workers, according to the report.

❸ Best Fitness Center, whose memberships was few and far between last month, now surprisingly transcends one of the best fitness centers in town.

❹ The aquarium is not specifically aimed at attracting marine biologists because it needs to make money.

❺ The town is heavily reliant on the export to make money, so local residents have to think other ways to transport the goods.

❶ 在 2010 年，面對著競爭對手，倍斯特手機開始失去了優勢，股價也因此而下跌。

❷ 由於無法找到外部的投資客資助，倍斯特服飾必須要裁減至少一萬名工人，根據報導。

❸ 在上個月，倍斯特健身中心的會員還相當稀少，現在卻出奇地超越了小鎮上其中一間最棒的健身中心。

❹ 水族館並未特別將目標放在吸引海洋生物學家，因為它要將其用於獲利。

❺ 小鎮高度仰賴出口來賺錢，所以當地居民必須要思考以其他方式來運送貨物。

⑥ Remaining extremely calm during confrontations is a good thing for the business deal.

⑦ Tourists in our garden can even visit our strawberry lab to test the freshness of the related product before they make a purchase.

⑧ During the period of the COVID-19 virus, Best Hotel admitted in the conference that the company encountered the greatest obstacle in 50 years, but it wanted to keep all employees employed.

⑨ Much of the time was spent finding evidence that can prove the client is actually innocent.

⑩ The CEO of Best Kitchen is now determined to get rid of lazy workers and employees who spread rumor about the company.

❻ 在爭執期間維持相當冷靜對於商業交易來說是件好事。

❼ 在購買前，花園的觀光客甚至可以參訪我們的草莓實驗室以檢測相關商品的新鮮度。

❽ 在新冠肺炎這段期間，倍斯特旅館在新聞記者會上坦承，公司遭遇了 50 年來最大的阻礙，但是會致力讓所有員工都能保有飯碗。

❾ 大多數時間都花費在尋找能夠證明客戶是真的清白的證據。

❿ 倍斯特廚房的執行長決定要除掉懶惰的工人和散布公司傳聞的員工。

❶ Because of multiple YouTubers' remarks about the new product, some consumers remain hesitant, thinking that they have to wait until the doubt is cleared up.

❷ Shoppers cannot let go of the snide comments made by bloggers, so they have made up their minds to unsubscribe a certain channel.

❸ Although the notoriety of the masseur has been widely known in the neighborhood, tourists traveling here are still kept in the dark.

❹ Due to a lack of evidence and recordings at the scene, the authenticity of the bad service made by the bank clerk cannot be verified.

❺ Despite the fact that the CFO of the Best Consulting firm has done numerous buy-ins of the stocks before, he still cannot say for sure whether the bet can truly generate hefty profits.

Part 1 單句中英互譯

Part 2 段落中譯英

Part 3 精選大作文

❶ 因為許多 YouTuber 對該新產品的評論，有些消費者對其仍舊持著猶豫的態度，認為必須要等到疑慮消除為止。

❷ 購物者們無法甩脫由部落客們所做的惡意評論，所以他們已經下定決心要退訂特定的頻道。

❸ 儘管男按摩師的惡名昭彰在整個街坊已經是廣為人知，到此地旅遊的觀光客們卻仍被蒙在鼓底。

❹ 由於缺乏現場的證據和記錄，銀行行員服務差的真實性是無法證實的。

❺ 儘管倍斯特顧問公司的財務長已經於之前從事過為數眾多的股市買進，他對於投注的賭注是否能真的產生鉅額的獲利仍無法說準。

6 A disgruntled employee is like a loose cannon, and can be quite detrimental to the work setting.

7 Disorganization on the shelves can be a downside for anyone walking in or clients visiting the warehouse.

8 In the aftermath of the 2009 financial crisis, numerous jobseekers experienced a shattered self-esteem and could not find the job for a few months.

9 Several start-ups can only afford an undersized warehouse and have to cut expenses in other areas, such as hiring and office equipment.

10 By undercutting the prices, Best Cinema is finally able to outcompete other movie studios and gets the chance to work with several celebrities.

❻ 憤恨不平的員工就像是一枚不定時炸彈，而且可能對於工作環境是危害甚鉅的。

❼ 對於任何走進倉庫或參訪的客戶來説，架上凌亂無章是個缺點。

❽ 在 2009 年金融危機後，許多求職者有著自尊受到粉碎的體驗，然後幾個月都無法找到工作。

❾ 幾個新創公司僅能夠負擔比普通小的倉庫，且必須要於其他項目，例如招聘和辦公室設備上刪減支出。

❿ 藉由削價競爭，倍斯特電影公司最終能夠勝過其他間電影工作室，並且有機會與幾位名人合作。

❶ Retention bonuses are needed in case the star employee wants to make a job hop and the company is not able to afford the loss.

❷ Situated in a secluded village where honey bees come to gather the honey near the river bank, Best Farm may be people's image of a stereotypical retreat.

❸ The winery in Germany has earned tons of accolades by tourists traveling very far from here.

❹ The dormancy in the area is a sign that the land cannot be too profitable, so buyers usually have doubts and look other places.

❺ Judging from the current circumstance, the animal doctor surmised that the wound of the koala could not be healed.

❶ 留任獎金是必須的，此舉能防備表現傑出的員工想要跳槽，而公司卻無法擔負這樣的損失。

❷ 座落於隱密的村莊，蜜蜂們都聚集在河岸邊採蜜，倍斯特農場可能是人們心中刻板印象隱密處的寫照。

❸ 位於德國的酒窖已經贏得了許多從遠處到訪的觀光客們的讚揚。

❹ 這個地區的休耕期是這塊土地無法太有利益價值的象徵，所以買家們通常存疑而改成瀏覽其他地方。

❺ 從現在的情況可以評判出，動物醫生臆測無尾熊的傷口是無法被治癒的。

⑥ Salespeople are known for their ability to sell, whereas editors are noted for their capability of editing articles.

⑦ The more you get to know the product, the more you can say during the product launch on next Wednesday.

⑧ Software developers are getting increasingly impatient with the questioning by salespeople, so the tension is a little high.

⑨ Because the company cannot afford to lose the CFO at the moment, the CEO finally agrees to give him a 10% raise.

⑩ The long-awaited promotion does not make the manager happy because the responsibility is greater than before.

❻ 銷售人員以他們的銷售能力而聞名，而編輯們則以他們的編輯文章的能力而著名。

❼ 你對於產品越是了解，在下週三的產品發佈期間就越有東西可以說。

❽ 軟體研發者對於銷售人員的質問漸漸地感到不耐煩，所以情勢是有點緊張的。

❾ 因為公司在這個當下是無法承受財務長的離開，所以執行長最終同意給予他 10% 的薪資增幅。

❿ 久盼的升遷並未使得經理感到開心，因為責任比起以往更加重了。

▶▶ UNIT 33 模擬試題（三十三）

❶ The lockdown of the city for a month has led to zero productivity and serenity of the street that are not usually seen in years.

❷ During the time of the outbreak of COVID-19 virus, bad things, such as layoffs and plant closure have become a regular scene.

❸ Singers and marine mammals are recruited to make the wedding more memorable and diverse, and the newlywed seems happy.

❹ Kitchen orders are usually enormous during the holiday, but with the invasion of the alien species, they are not as large as it used to be.

❺ Our fruits and vegetables are under such an extensive care that they are put in an artificial setting where temperatures are rigorously monitored.

❶ 封城一個月已經導致生產力歸零且街道的寧靜是這幾年來不尋常的景象。

❷ 在新冠肺炎病毒爆發的期間，壞事例如解雇和工廠結束營業已經成了常景。

❸ 歌手們和海洋哺乳類動物都受僱，讓婚宴更有回憶性且多樣化，而新婚夫妻對此似乎感到樂此不疲。

❹ 在假日期間，廚房的訂單通常很大筆，但是隨著外來種的入侵，訂單沒有往常那麼多了。

❺ 我們的水果和蔬菜受到那樣的完善照護以致於它們被放置於溫度受到嚴密監控的人工環境裡。

⑥ Unlike most cellphone giants, which outsource software components to other low-cost countries, Best Cellphone is doing quite the opposite.

⑦ A few of the candidates we interviewed acknowledged that they had had at least 5 job hops before finding the right one.

⑧ Even though male dates vary considerably in different occupations, your intuition and criteria for a mate can narrow candidates down to the most suitable one.

⑨ Best Chocolate Plant's remarkable growth in profits has allured multiple overseas investors and sponsors.

⑩ If the productivity of Best Automobile drops 10%, the overall revenue will decrease at least 50 million dollars.

Part 1 單句中英互譯

Part 2 段落中譯英

Part 3 精選大作文

❻ 不像大多數的手機大廠，將軟體組件外包到其他低成本的國家，倍斯特手機卻是反其道而行。

❼ 我們面試過的幾位候選人承認在找到合適的工作之前，他們有至少五次的職涯跑道轉換。

❽ 儘管男性約會對象在不同職業中有顯著地不同，你的直覺和對男性的標準能夠將候選人窄化至最合適的那位。

❾ 倍斯特巧克力廠驚人的利潤成長已經吸引了眾多的海外投資者和贊助者。

❿ 如果倍斯特汽車的生產下降 10%，整體收入會減少至少 5 千萬元。

這個 part 輔以「段落中譯英」練習，在養成寫單一句子後，循序漸進練習段落翻譯，並對照參考答案檢視自我能力，寫出邏輯嚴謹的層層推論，讓論點環環相扣且更具說服力。

PART 2

UNIT 01 升學考試的壓力、備考艱辛、書商利益

 段落中譯英 ▶ *MP3 001*

　　我之所以會支持傳統使用統一標準教科書的教學方式，可總結至一個大方向論點，在於：位在我們所建立的教育體系下的社經環境；首先，在如台灣的亞洲社會裡，要在升學考試中表現亮眼的壓力是無法粉碎的。在此情況下，因為學生無法清楚地歸納出考試範圍，他們在準備考試的過程，將會備感艱辛；第二，學校進而發展出一套新的挑選教科書機制，且是個以商業為導向的機制，因其擁有充分的決定權，可各自挑選偏好的教科書廠商，但學校很可能著眼於廠商私下所保證的個人商業利益，而犧牲了學生的普遍權益，尤其當政府未盡到應盡的責任監督時，檯面下的交易更是普遍，至今政府也尚未推出有效的防治機制。

_____

_____

_____

_____

_____

_____

【參考答案】

The reasons why I support the traditional way of learning with standardized textbooks can be boiled down to one common theme: the socio-economic environment where the education system is built upon. First, in an Asian society such as Taiwan, the pressure of performing outstandingly on national exams for senior high school is unshakable. In this scenario, students inevitably suffer stress while preparing for those entrance exams, as no boundaries of test materials can be clearly drawn. Secondly, a new kind of mechanism for deciding which published textbooks to go with is hatched, and it has become a commercial one. Schools now have the freedom to choose their own preferred textbooks, and the decisions made can be based upon commercial benefits between schools and publishers, not in the best interests of pupils. This kind of under-table agreements will be particularly prevalent without proper government supervision, and we have not seen relevant counter mechanisms from the government for now.

Part 1 單句中英互譯

Part 2 段落中譯英

Part 3 精選大作文

UNIT 02

蓬勃發展的術科、義務教育、社經差距

 段落中譯英 ▶ *MP3 002*

在 9 年國教多年後，不僅傳統所注重的學科為教學重點，近年來蓬勃發展的術科也越來越受到重視。換句話說，原本的體系早已開始提供不同興趣取向的學生們發展的舞台，而他們所最不需要的，即是一個會帶來劇變、混亂及困惑的新體系；此外，12 年國教所倡導的「將高中職3 年融入義務教育將縮小社經差距」是沒有根據的，不是所有人都適合追求與學術相關的職業，而社會的整體運作也並不需要所有人都追求學術，而若要改善年輕學子誤入歧途的機率，協助他們加入實習計畫，也會比強制他們留在校園內來得有效，這樣一來，他們不僅能在實習工作上學習相關經驗，也能夠賺取相對的報酬，這對於社會結構的平衡及縮小社經差距將更有效果。

_____

_____

_____

_____

_____

_____

【參考答案】

Over the years, the system had actually morphed into something where the once highly-held academic subjects were caught up by the growing popularity of vocational skills and experiences. In other words, the original system had created a space where students that are differently inclined can all find places to further their interests, either academic or vocational. The last thing it needed is a new system that brings drastic changes, chaos and confusion. Furthermore, such a claim as stating the extra mandated 3 years of education can narrow social gaps is ungrounded. Not everyone is built to pursue an academic related career path, nor does the society need so. Besides, one of the best ways to learn is through hands-on experiences, and it can be more productive for youngsters, who are in risk of potentially going off course, to enter paid programs for internship than forcing them to stay in school. This way, they learn on the job, and are able to earn income, both of which conducive to a more balanced social structure, and hence more effectively narrow social gaps.

UNIT 03　考試的成績與畢業後的成就的關連性

段落中譯英　▶ *MP3 003*

　　首先，自古至今有許多並沒有畢業於所謂的明星學校，但在各界發展極為成功的人士們。舉傑米・奧利佛的例子來說，這位明星主廚在小時候被診斷出患有閱讀障礙，無法快速理解書面上的意思，但仍在競爭激烈的料理界闖出一片天，可見很多時候，考試的成績與畢業後的成就並沒有絕對的關連性；第二，考試的範圍，往往侷限於測試學生個體的背誦技能，而無法激發學生深入、全面性地去探討某學科範圍，而這種體制，孤立了不善考試，但卻擁有其它天賦的學生，但這些學生真不應該因為不善考試，而受到不平等對待。

_____

_____

_____

_____

_____

_____

【參考答案】

First and foremost, there have been countless examples of people who do not graduate from the top of school rankings, but are still tremendously successful in their choice of path. Take Jamie Oliver for example, the celebrity chef, who was early diagnosed with dyslexia, a disease preventing him from comprehending written words in a smooth manner, still manages to have all the success in the world in the competitive industry of culinary craftsmanship. This goes to show that how individuals perform in school tests has no absolute connection with their success after graduation. Secondly, examinations are oftentimes only capable of testing individuals' certain areas of capabilities, such as one's short-term memory. This type of test system isolates those who are endowed with other talents than doing exceptionally well on academic tests. They should also have the opportunity to be celebrated for their talents despite the fact that these talents might have nothing to do with taking a test.

UNIT 04 技職體系、「唯有讀書高」的觀念

 段落中譯英 ▶ *MP3 004*

　　根據這個思維，我贊同某些特定的學生應有選擇自己受教育方式的權利，並因而發展得更好，因為有些學生天生適合藉由實際的經驗來學習，正如有些學生天生適合藉由書籍、理論來學習，而對於那些能夠在技職體系出類拔萃的學生們，理所當然地他們應該避免進入一般高中體系，以避免浪費時間在對於畢業後的工作無實質影響的事物上。另外，由於現在社會逐漸不像以前持有「唯有讀書高」的觀念，技職教育在現今的社會環境下，反而與一般高中體系一樣被重視。

【參考答案】

Along this line of thinking, I agree and believe that for a certain group of students, they should have the freedom to choose which kind of education they receive, and thus better off from that choice. The reason is that some students are wired to learn through physical experiences, the same as the fact that some students are born to comprehend faster through books and theories. For those students who will thrive in vocational schools, they should just avoid wasting time at traditional senior high schools, but should rather learn practical skills at a vocational school. The other reason lies in the gradual change of social perception where people do not hold academic achievements in as high a regard as in the past. Instead, vocational education is, in today's social climate, given the same weight as the traditional general education.

UNIT 05 扭曲的教學方式、獲益良多的事

 段落中譯英 ▶ *MP3 005*

　　直至今日，教育體系其極不均衡的著重在學生的考試能力，而不是著重在學生如何真正瞭解手邊的教學科目上，是讓人驚恐的。而這種扭曲的教學方式是偏離根本的，因其導致學生花費許多精力在學習如何於考試中取得高分，花費較少精力在瞭解各個學科背後的知識，而學生或許也會認為接受補習班的幫助會是件獲益良多的事，尤其是在學習如何考試取得高分的「藝術」上，但這種認知上的獲益，很快就會被消磨掉，尤其當學生脫離考試的階段後，開始進入至人生另一個環節，學生們無法避免地將發現到，真正去瞭解一個學科的知識，將會比學習如何考試來的重要。

_____

_____

_____

_____

_____

_____

_____

【參考答案】

As of today, the disproportionate focus placed on test taking skills of students, rather than a real understanding of subject matters at hand, is alarming. This kind of distorted approach to imparting knowledge is way off base, as students concentrate too much energy on how to acquire higher exam scores, but spend less energy on developing actual interest in each subject. In the short run, students might consider it beneficial for them to receive a helping hand with test-taking, which is warmly extended by cram school operators to assist with the masterful "art" of scoring excellent marks on tests. However, these perceived benefits can easily wear off once students pass the phase of exam-taking, and enter the stage of life where, inevitably, they are faced with a world where a true understating of a subject matter will be more importantly weighed upon than how well you can take a test in that subject matter.

UNIT 06
學習能力、均質的環境

 段落中譯英 ▶ *MP3 006*

　　通常來說，教育體制有義務來確保對所有的利益相關者，主要是學生，提供一個公平學習的環境，但也必須照顧到某些與同學齡相比，有才華、且能力出眾的學生盡情學習的平台，因他們的特殊才華，本身就注定會比同儕表現的還要亮眼；若這些在某些學科表現特別出眾的學生與普通學習能力的學生一起上課，前者可能會容易分心，進而影響到他們極力開發自己潛能的機會，但相反地，若是這些資質優異的學生與同等級的學生一起上課，將非常有可能會產生不同的結果，因此，幸好有「資優班」的誕生，提供了程度較好的學生在一個與自己實力相當、均質的環境學習的機會。

_____

_____

_____

_____

_____

_____

【參考答案】

Generally speaking, the education system has the responsibility to ensure not only a level playing field for all parties involved, mainly the students, but also a place for those naturally gifted, especially those that are endowed with capabilities are bound to stand out more than their equal counterparts. In a situation where students considered top of the notch in certain areas of study are mixed with students that are not blessed in the same design, the former run the risk of being easily distracted. This will in turn deter those with ample aptitude from what they are able to achieve, and it would have been a different story only if these students in question were to learn in such an environment that is a match to the level of their intellectual charge. Thankfully, the "Gifted Class" provides the exact place that is homogenous, a place where students can expect to be educated and learn amongst people with similar aptitude and benchmarked the same.

UNIT 07

「有教無類」、受教育的權利

 段落中譯英 ▶ *MP3 007*

　　首先，如俗話所說的，「有教無類」，若天生有學習困難的孩子，不應該被處罰，更不應該被剝奪教育的權利，而因為一般的傳統教室學習環境，對他們來說並不是有助益、滋養的環境，所以政府至少應提供給這些孩子一個健康的、適宜的替代方案；第二點，教育對於這些孩子來說是個嚴肅的議題，因為若沒有適當的教育，他們或許連照顧自身基本的需求都有問題，這就是為什麼我們身為社會大家庭的一份子，應對於這些「資源班」的孩子更加包容才是。

_____

_____

_____

_____

_____

_____

_____

【參考答案】

First of all, as the saying goes, "Education is a right, not a privilege." Those who are born with learning disabilities should not be punished, let alone to be stripped of their right to education. As it would not be a conducive and nurturing environment for them to go through learning at a conventional classroom setting, the least government can do is to provide a healthy, appropriate alternative for them. Secondly, education is an especially serious matter to those with learning disabilities, as without education, they might not be able to even sustain or maintain their basic life needs. That is why we, the society as an agglomerate of humanity, should be more inclusive towards those who study in a "Resource Room."

UNIT
08
批判性思考、出社會

 段落中譯英 ▶ *MP3 008*

　　首先，教育的最終目標，應該是幫助學生能夠做好未來進入社會的準備，而在現實生活中，人們必須靠批判性思考來做許多決定，因為其實並沒有真正的一套準則來告訴大家人生中正確的道路怎麼走，尤其畢業後的現實人生是很複雜的，並不像在學校考試一樣，有一定的選項可以選擇。現實人生需要廣泛地思考，並需要依據各種狀況來做不同的判斷，並批判性地來評斷各種決定可能會造成的結果才行。

_____

_____

_____

_____

_____

_____

【參考答案】

For starters, the ultimate goal for education should be to better prepare students for the real world so that they are bound to enter at some point in their lives. In real life, people need to make decisions based on critical thinking, as there is rarely a firm set of guidelines that tell people which path is the correct one to embark on, or which footsteps are the right ones to follow in, especially in relation to dealing with something as complicated in nature as life is. Life after graduation is not as simple as taking a test, where spaces are to be filled with multiple choices; it requires extensive thinking, and it requires people to make a series of decisions based off of their judgment on the general situation, the nuances that differ in each situation, and to critically evaluate each outcome that comes along with each decision made.

UNIT 09 現實社會的縮影、篤志好學

段落中譯英 ▶ *MP3 009*

　　學校教育其中的一個優點，就是讓學生有與各種個性的同學互動、交流的機會，而學校可說是現實社會的縮影，在現實社會中，與人互動的技巧是非常重要的。而自學教育剝奪了孩子學習此項技能的機會，不論這些孩子是多麼地篤志好學，他們都需要親身去體驗怎麼交朋友，如何在團體中生活等等，而之所以會稱為社交「技能」，指的就是必須做中學，不是僅僅藉由閱讀就可以學會的。

_____

_____

_____

_____

_____

_____

_____

【參考答案】

One of the advantages for education at school is to have the opportunity presented to students to interact and mingle with all kinds of personalities. Schools may be considered a microcosm of the real world, where interpersonal skills are an integral part of everyday life. Home schooling strips children of such opportunities. No matter how much these children have a mind like a steel trap, they all need to experience interpersonal relationships firsthand to figure out and learn how to make friends with others and how they are going to fit in a group setting. As it is called "interpersonal skills," students need to learn from their actual experiences of interacting with others.

UNIT 10　「芝蘭之室」、「胎教」

段落中譯英　▶ MP3 010

　　在人生的各個階段中，身旁的環境，當接觸一定的時間後，對我們的言行舉止有很大的影響是不可否認的，也就是成語「芝蘭之室」所描述的情形。這句成語加強了有關外在環境對我們影響的論述，不論那外在環境是正面還是負面的，而在剛接觸新環境的時候，我們理所當然會對身邊某些人事物的特質非常敏感，但時間久了之後，我們也將對這些特質漸漸習慣、麻木，而尚未出生的胎兒何嘗不是如此呢？尤其胎兒是處在人生中最易受影響的階段之一，因為他們還在生長、成形中，而有關「胎教」的一些有趣的方法，包括了對著媽媽的肚子播放古典音樂，或是媽媽經常、規律性地瀏覽藝術作品、美麗的照片等等。

【參考答案】

Throughout all stages of human life, there is no denying that the environment around us would have a huge impact on what kind of person we turn out to be. As the saying goes, "When you lie down with dogs, you will get up with fleas." This old adage reinforces the idea that outer influences, whether positive or negative, all have their individual effects on us. Human beings are used to picking up habits when they are exposed to certain kinds of behavior long enough. So why would it be any different for them in the prenatal stage, one of the most impressionable stages of human beings as we are still forming and developing during pregnancy. Some interesting ways to "Prenatal Education" are to play classical music to mothers' bellies, or ask mothers to regularly browse through art pieces and beautiful pictures, and so on.

UNIT 11

「梧鼠技窮」、領域專精

 段落中譯英 ▶ *MP3 011*

　　正如成語「梧鼠技窮」所形容的，其也完美詮釋出負荷過重、繁忙學生們的心聲。此外，孩子們課外才藝班的課程安排，以及孩子們所能享有的自由時間、能夠盡情地玩耍，其中的平衡是很難拿捏的。不幸的是，家長總是給孩子太多負荷，要求他們參加過多的才藝班，如運動、樂器演奏、手工藝等課程，而結果就是學生們在各個他們被逼迫學習的領域中淺度學習、接觸，但都不是很專精，而這個結果必定不是大家所樂見的，還不如給孩子們多一點喘息的空間，是比較有幫助的。

【參考答案】

As the saying goes, "Jack of all trades, master of none." This saying perfectly embodies the sentiment behind overburdened students who have been spread too thin. Besides, the balance between the number of talent classes that children need to attend and the free time reserved for them to just be children is often hard to define. Unfortunately, children are found to be overloaded with way too many courses. Children have to attend sports classes, learn how to play musical instruments, develop artistic interests through craftsmanship workshops, and the list goes on. As a result, children have no choice but to be dabbling in, rather than to become an expert of everything that they are forced to come in contact with. This outcome is certainly not desired by both parents and children, and it would be much more beneficial for parents to cut their children some slack.

 段落中譯英 ▶ *MP3 012*

　　首先,「關聯性學習法」指的是鼓勵學生將某一方面的所學應用、延伸至其它可應用的範圍的教學方法。換句話說,學生被教導、訓練以觸類旁通的方式,來更有效率地學習,而在語言學習的競技場中,日文就是個很好的例子,雖然它與英文可謂發源於地球上的兩個極端,但因歷史及貿易的發展,它們享有許多相似的字詞,而今日的語言學習者應當善加利用此方便性,來更加有效率地學習世界各種語言。

【參考答案】

First of all, "learning by association" describes the teaching methodology where students are encouraged to apply what they have learned to other areas of study. In other words, pupils are taught and trained to connect the dots of various disciplines so that they are flexible enough to absorb knowledge in a much more efficient way. As in the arena of language learning, one example can be found in the language of Japanese, whose words share the same roots with the English language, despite the fact that Japan and other English-speaking countries are geographically far apart. This phenomenon can be explained by human history and the involvement of international trade, and learners of language today ought to utilize such convenience to their best advantage in order to learn world languages in a much more productive way.

UNIT 13 工作評鑑、裙帶關係

 段落中譯英 ▶ *MP3 013*

　　多年來，政府對於底下公務員所施行的工作表現評鑑的方法備受爭議，許多評論家認為這些評鑑方法不夠透明，不是純粹由個人的工作表現來評鑑，且評鑑者還不需為自己所給予的評鑑負責。另外，公務員本身的工作範圍、權責，與政治幕後的操作很密切，也因此裙帶關係難以杜絕，所以任人唯才的施政難以落實；因此，我主張改善公務員效率的第一步，就是政府應當根本地改革目前所實施的工作評鑑方針，改為透明、用人唯才的評鑑方法。正如生於憂患，死於安樂所述，公務員在適當的獎懲壓力下，才會提升工作效率，並且，他們在較公平的工作評鑑制度下，也才更有可能自發上進，在工作表現上努力。

_____

_____

_____

_____

_____

_____

【參考答案】

For years, the governmental ways to conduct performance reviews on public servants have been much criticized by critics as not being transparent, not based on meritocracy, and not holding the reviewers accountable for their given-out performance audits. Also, as closely involved as public servants are with their inner workings with politics, nepotism is not easy to completely rid of, making the practice of meritocracy much harder to implement. Hence, I propose the first step to improve public servant's work efficiency is to overhaul the current performance review methods to a more transparent, merit based one. As diamonds are made under pressure, public servants will increase efficiency if they are properly pressured and incentivized. Besides, if public servants are subject to a fairer method of performance audit, they would be more inclined to strive for a better work performance as well.

UNIT 14 學生數量短缺、大學文憑的可信度

段落中譯英 ▶ *MP3 014*

　　首先，當台灣的生育率持續下滑，且沒有好轉的跡象時，將會造成日後學生數的短缺，這將嚴重威脅到剩餘的大學，因為大家都知道，大學的營運就如同企業一樣，都需要資金及相當的資源以求生存，而即將出現的學生數量短缺也代表了學費、資金的短缺，最終將迫使許多大學別無選擇而倒閉。另外，過多的高等教育學府將使入學變得過於簡易，反而使社會對於畢業大學生的期望降低，也將對於大學文憑的可信度產生質疑。

_____

_____

_____

_____

_____

_____

【參考答案】

For starters, as the birth rates in Taiwan have been declining, and show no sign of pace in any foreseeable future, there will soon be a shortage of students. This is a real threat to many of those redundant colleges and universities as it is no secret that the running of educational institutions is very much alike the running of business conglomerates as they both indeed need monetary resources in order to last for long. Hence, the incoming shortage of students means that a shortage of tuition fees, and college and universities have no choice but to close down. Moreover, the abundance of higher educational institutions will lead to an overly easy access for students who will probably not need to work as hard as otherwise required to get into colleges and universities, which will then result in lowered expectations of college graduates and decreased credibility of college diplomas.

UNIT 15　碩士教育、研究所的廣泛增設

段落中譯英 ▶ *MP3 015*

　　首先，我們必須了解碩士教育的重點在於學術的探討。然而，許多台灣人將碩士學位的取得與職場工作的表現視為同一件事，而當台灣的許多企業在徵才時只考慮有碩士學位的求職者時，令人感到格外地諷刺。因為這些取得碩士學位的學生們，花了許多時間在學術的訓練上，但對於他們學位專科在現實生活中的運用，並沒有相對應的熟稔度，若不是要成為學者，或純粹地想要更深入探討某一學科領域，攻讀碩士學位或許並不如台灣社會所想的，並不是對於將知識應用於現實生活中般有幫助的；第二，為了應付攻讀研究所的需求，研究所的廣泛增設，將使攻讀研究所這件事平凡化，而最終也將使攻讀研究所流於形式，只因為大家都在讀。最後，因為許多大學畢業生還無法知道自己的興趣為何，所以大學畢業生應當在現實世界中多加嘗試，在更瞭解自己的性向、興趣之後，再回去攻讀也不遲。

【參考答案】

First, it is important to understand that the purpose of postgraduate education is supposed to be about academic exploration. However, many Taiwanese view someone's completion of a postgraduate degree synonymous with someone being workplace ready. It is especially ironic as many business entities in Taiwan only give out interview opportunities to candidates with master's degrees. It is ironic because those who spend much time completing a master's degree are mostly academically trained rather than well-versed in the real-world operations of whichever specialization they are exploring. As a matter of fact, years of academic studies towards garnering a master's degree may not truly benefit individuals in the long run, unless their career aspiration is to become an established scholar in their chosen fields of study. Secondly, the increase in the supply of graduate schools to meet the corresponding demand will make the process of finishing graduate programs less special, and soon graduating from a postgraduate school will just be a formality since everyone else is doing the same without great difficulty. Lastly, college graduates are often unsure as to what their real interests are, and graduates should test the waters in the real world and get back to school for postgraduate studies when they have a better gauge on their interests.

UNIT 16
職場與學校的教育的不同

 段落中譯英 ▶ MP3 016

　　正如生活中的許多事物，兵在精，不在多。然而，當社會多年來盲目地高估高等教育對學生所帶來的益處時，人們容易有個錯誤的觀念，認為教育在學生日後的職涯發展、成功上，扮演了不可或缺的角色，但許多年輕人並未及早發覺職場與學校的教育是很不同的，因為很多時候，攀爬企業階級所需要的是實務經驗，而不是靠一個人的學歷背景。根據以上論述，簡單來說，一個人的學歷多寡，還不如其所受的教育品質，也就是他們對於進入社會、職場的準備程度還來得重要，因此，我反對台灣社會對於教育多寡過度著重的現象。

_____

_____

_____

_____

_____

_____

【參考答案】

As with many things in life, quality over quantity is the way to go. However, as the society has been for years blindly overestimating the benefits that come with higher education, people are easily given the wrong impression of how educations play such an integral role in determining how well of they are going to be when entering the job market. They, especially youngsters, are not aware of how it is a whole new ball game when they are starting a career. Oftentimes, you need to work yourself up the corporate ladder on the merits of practical experience, rather than one's education background. In short, with the above said, I feel the amount of education is not as important as its quality, in terms of how well people are properly trained and prepared for the real world. Thus, I oppose the overstated hype placed on the amount of education by the Taiwanese society.

UNIT 17 瞭解企業的運作方式

段落中譯英 ▶ *MP3 017*

　　首先，任何的經驗皆是好的經驗，端看個人如何內化自身的經驗，並擷取出對於日後人生中無可避免的挑戰，些許有用的心得及感想。而也因為學校的環境與社會險惡的環境差距甚遠，他們更應該盡量接觸、探索瞭解企業的運作方式，以及商務人士於專業情境中應如何互動等等。當然，不可能所有的實習經驗都是正面、美好的，尤其當實習生的給配是如此微薄時。但是，能夠在負面經驗中擷取正面學習經驗的學生，仍是能在最後帶走寶貴的經驗。

_____

_____

_____

_____

_____

_____

_____

【參考答案】

To begin with, any experience is good experience. It is up to individuals to internalize whatever situations they find themselves in, and extract something useful from them to go with so that they are better prepared when later on inevitably facing challenges in life. As the school environment is vastly different from the cut throat business world, they should really get themselves exposed, and gain first-hand insights into how businesses operate, how people interact with each other in a professional setting, and so on. Granted, not all experiences would be pleasant, especially when monetary rewards for these internship positions are typically minimal. Still, those who make lemonade out of lemons can still bring invaluable lessons from which they are in touch with during their internship programs.

UNIT 18　跳脫舒適圈、「讀萬卷書，行萬里路」

段落中譯英 ▶ MP3 018

　　目前的情況有兩個方面值得討論：金錢及充實人生經歷的體驗，如在上段所提及的，打工度假機會所提供的金錢酬勞是很龐大的，當然於工作上所付出的精力也是相對辛苦的。然而，除了金錢，那些嘗試打工度假的人常發現他們的視野開闊了，因為打工度假讓他們必須跳脫舒適圈，且當在國外時，他們會經歷許多不熟悉、沒聽過，甚至是從沒想過會發生的事情，而當在國外面對無預期的挑戰時，他們必須依靠自己。這些，無庸置疑地，將使他們從這些充實人生經歷的體驗中成長。綜合上述，諺語說的「讀萬卷書，行萬里路」似乎是真的。那些選擇讓打工度假成為他們人生旅途中之一的景點的人，正是此諺語的最佳驗證，因此我支持、鼓勵人們嘗試打工度假。

_____

_____

_____

_____

_____

_____

【參考答案】

There are two aspects to this situation: one is monetary and the other would be life-enriching experiences. As mentioned in the last paragraph, the monetary rewards of working holiday opportunities are usually tremendous, although it goes without saying that these rewards are earned through hard work as well. Also, people can broaden their horizons when working in foreign, unfamiliar countries. When abroad, they are exposed to many things that are unfamiliar, unheard of, or not even thought of. What's more, they need to depend on themselves when facing unexpected challenges in a foreign country. All these, without a doubt, will ultimately contribute to growth that is derived from these life-enriching experiences. With Above-mentioned arguments combined, it seems that the saying "he that travels far knows much" is true. Those who have chosen working holiday opportunities as part of their life course are the true testament to this saying, and that is why I support people taking actions on this.

UNIT 19
事情雪上加霜、模仿效應

 段落中譯英 ▶ *MP3 019*

　　首先，台灣最近有一連串於公開場合殺人的事件，而當這些罪犯並沒有於逮捕後的第一時間處以相關責任刑罰時，不只使事情雪上加霜，也產生了模仿效應。自從第一起隨機殺人事件發生後，隨後發生的類似案件可被視為第一起案件的副產物，而事實上，許多人譴責司法系統所缺乏的即時處罰、判決機制，造就了這波模仿效應。因此，我們必須瞭解到，若單純司法處罰、判決的延遲，就能夠對於整個社會產生許多影響，那死刑的廢除更是不用說了。

_____

_____

_____

_____

_____

_____

_____

【參考答案】

To begin with, there have been a couple of incidents where manslaughter is carried out in the broad daylight in Taiwan. The fact that the criminals responsible are not executed immediately after arrest is not only adding insult to injury, but also creating the Imitation Effect. Since the first incident of random killing took place, the following episodes of similar offences are considered a byproduct of the first incidence. In fact, many people actually blame the Imitation Effect a result of the legal system's lack of warranted punishment on the first offender in a timely manner. Therefore, it is important to point out that since the pure delay of proper execution on offenders could have ramifications on the whole society, the abolition of the death penalty is for sure to have a bigger impact.

UNIT
20

「己所不欲，勿施於人」

 段落中譯英 ▶ *MP3 020*

　　首先，儘管許多反對的聲浪因宗教信仰而加劇，諷刺的是聖經中卻倡導著「己所不欲，勿施於人」的觀念。而這個觀念也正是我支持同性婚姻合法化的原因，正如異性戀個體正當享受與另一半合法結婚的權益，若被剝奪此權益將會感到極度沮喪。因此，LGBT 社群個體也應當享有相同的權益；第二點，科學家還無法確切地瞭解性傾向的影響因素，有些推測性傾向是由基因所決定的，而因為天生的性傾向而遭剝奪相關的權益是不公平的。

【參考答案】

First of all, despite the fact that much of the opposition is fueled by religious beliefs, it is ironic that the quote "Do unto others as you would have them do unto you" comes straight from the bible. This quote essentially explains why I stand in favor of the legalization of same-sex marriages, as heterosexual individuals much enjoy their given right to legally marry their significant others and would be much upset if stripped of that given privilege. In that thread of thought, individuals from the LGBT community should enjoy the same. Secondly, it is not scientifically conclusive as to why individuals are attracted to the same sex. Some posit that sexual orientations are genetically determined, and it is unfair to be stripped of their legal right based on the way they are born and brought to the world.

UNIT 21 少子化的現象、「衣食足而後禮義興」

段落中譯英 ▶ *MP3 021*

　　有關世界各地少子化的現象，我並不秉持負面的觀點，反而，我認為整體社會應當好好考量當面對此議題時，該如何面對？畢竟，當整體來說，世界越加走向已開發、文明的發展時，少子化的趨勢是很難逆轉的。因此，社會應對少子化的方式是極度重要的，而我也認為，若能夠於此時把握因少子化趨勢而衍生出來的機會，整體社會福祉將能夠改善、提升。正如諺語「衣食足而後禮義興」所說的，當生活水準與社會、國家的發展一同提升時，生活水平將發展至一定的境界，而過往、古早時代較為節省的生活方式將難以被新世代接受，而少子化的現象也將減少各個家庭的負擔，因為孩子們不必再跟兄弟姊妹爭取家庭裡有限的資源。

【參考答案】

When it comes to discussions pertaining to the developing trend in declining birth rates around the world, I do not hold a negative view on such an issue. Rather, I think it is how the society, as a whole, deals with such an issue that should be taken into serious considerations. After all, as the world is collectively getting more developed and civilized over the passage of time, the trend in declining birth rates shall turn out to be irreversible. As a result, how societies respond to fewer children being born to the world is of paramount importance. What's more, I think there are quite a few timely opportunities that can be taken advantage of during this period for the progression of society as a whole. As the saying goes, "First comes food then morality." As the level of living standards are lifted with the development of countries and societies, a certain kind of life style has come into place that would not be easily replaced by the older ways of living; that is, a more frugal way. Fewer children being born can lessen economic burdens on families. In turn, they can then have more access to available resources in the family, with no need to share or divide those resources with siblings.

UNIT 22 「乏人問津」、營運市場競爭激烈

 段落中譯英 ▶ *MP3 022*

　　舉例來說，若一個企業的主要業務為銷售嬰兒用品，這個企業幾年後未來的前景將如何呢？當社會中的出生率下降、社會平均年齡上升，這個假設的企業很有可能會被淘汰，倘若其不做出即時、適當的改變的話；換句話說，這個企業最後於市場上將會乏人問津，因為老化的人口多半會對於嬰兒用品毫無興趣。因此，企業改變及調整策略將是生存之道。總結來說，企業營運是艱難的，而營運市場總是變化萬千、競爭激烈，上演著適者生存的遊戲，而最好的應變方式，或許就是於編制年度計畫時，開始將高齡市場納入考量範圍內。

_____

_____

_____

_____

_____

_____

【參考答案】

For example, if a business is now mainly in baby amenities business, what the prospects are going to look like after a few years passing? As the birth rates are just ever going to be on a downward slope, whereas the age average for society demographics is on an upward slope, the hypothetical business would most likely to go under if it does not react quickly enough to the aging component of the business environment. In other words, this business would go begging as elders would find no use for baby amenities. Therefore, adaptation and changing tactics for businesses are the strongly recommended. In conclusion, running a business is tough, and the market place is always fickle and fierce for the game of the survival of the fittest. The best tactic for businesses may be to start incorporating senior customers into considerations when devising annual market strategies.

UNIT 23 安樂死的合法化

段落中譯英 ▶ *MP3 023*

在某些特定健康方面的條件下，我支持個體應有法律保障，有權決定是否要對自身實施安樂死。就以台灣來說，有許多的案例為病患只能倚靠各種醫療器材來苟延壽命，但在長遠的未來中，卻無法實際地復原、恢復，對於病患本身來說，他們多半表示無意願以這種方式延長壽命，而對於病患家屬來說，他們也必須承受累積昂貴的醫療費用，也必須花費許多體力、精力。因此，在這種情況下，我贊同安樂死的合法化，因為若只是純粹用器材延長壽命，讓病患只是純粹施行最基本的生理功能，如呼吸、吸收流質食物等，是沒有意義的。

【參考答案】

I support for individuals' right to legally undergo euthanasia under dire conditions, especially in terms of one's health issues. Take Taiwan for example, there are many instances where many patients are clinically sustained with all kinds of medical instruments but without prospect of recovery in the near future. For one, these sustained patients themselves oftentimes express no desire of prolonging their lives that way, and for another, these accumulated medical expenses are endured by the rest of the family, who not only exhaust much money but also physical and mental strength on such sustaining. In these kinds of cases, I think euthanasia should be legalized as there is literally no point of sustaining a body who only performs the basic bodily functions, such as breathing, absorbing fluid foods, etc.

UNIT 24 「分庭抗禮」、性傾向

段落中譯英 ▶ *MP3 024*

　　在人生中的各個領域，有許多代表 LGBT 社群的榮耀人物，舉例來說，在奧運比賽數度奪冠的游泳選手伊恩・索普，即是個公開承認自己性傾向的選手，而伊恩的例子也證明了 LGBT 的社群代表，在許多方面是能夠與傳統二元男女性別分法的代表一樣優秀、分庭抗禮的。因此，若 LGBT 社群無法享有應有的平等權益，而無法培育、訓練出如伊恩般優秀的選手時，其對於社會及國家的損失將可想而知，因為他們若被法律歧視、或是被社會不合理對待，將可能無法在其專業領域中表現傑出，而社會及國家因而失去如伊恩般優秀的冠軍選手是很可惜的。

【參考答案】

In many areas of life, there are quite a few illustrious representations on behalf of the LGBT community, such as Ian Thorpe and others. Ian Thorpe now is an openly gay athlete who has won numerous Olympic swimming champion titles. This example illustrates the fact that, in many ways, representatives of the LGBT community can hold a candle to representatives of the traditionally defined sexes: male and female. We only need to think about the potential loss if we do not provide people like Ian get deserved equal rights. They might not have the chance to excel at what they do if they are discriminated against by the law or are treated unfairly by the society, and that would be a shame for societies to lose the honor brought upon by life champions like Ian Thorpe.

UNIT 25

中年失業、「時不我予」

　　首先，高齡失業的族群，因為人生也走了大半部分，因此也經歷了較多的人生起伏，而也因為如此，他們能藉由自身的經驗，於工作職場上應對自如，而這些技能是很重要的。因為在職場上，很多時候與人相處的學問比個人的專業技能還要來得重要；另外，別忘了，每個挑戰的背後都是另一個機會，儘管對於中年失業、轉業的員工來說，挑戰縱然極困難，但也不是完全沒有機會，正如成語「時不我予」所傳達的，在當下來看，往日的時間、機會已過，然而應盡快調整心態，將注意力集中在新技能的學習，而不是沉溺在過去，才是有生產力的。

【參考答案】

For starters, people of relatively older ages have for sure lived a longer life, have gone through more ups and downs of what life brings. As a result, they have much more life experiences, which they can easily draw upon, for all different kinds of work situations. Oftentimes at the work place, knowing how to deal with people is even more important than one's specialized skills. Also, do not forget that every challenge is an opportunity, and despite the fact that it will be exceptionally challenging for people of middle ages to switch careers, it is not entirely impossible. As the saying goes, "Lost time is never found again." It would be much more productive to keep learning new skills to prove one's value for prospective employers, than to keep mulling over the lost time.

UNIT 26 失控的房價、稅賦

 段落中譯英 ▶ *MP3 026*

　　首先，台灣政府對於失控的房價採取相關應對措施只是遲早的問題。對於許多房地產商來說，他們的目標是將利潤最大化、蠶食鯨吞地將可賺取的利益到手，而儘管在某一層面上來說，企業賺取利益原本就是他們應有的權益，但當他們不擇手段，並對於被其行為所影響的其它人毫無同理心時，就是個不一樣的狀況了，這不僅對於整個社會來說是毫無責任感的，且是個資本主義扭曲、變形的經典例子，所以，政府的確應當出手，藉由修改稅賦來適當調整失控的狀況。

【參考答案】

To begin with, it is just a sooner-or-later matter for governments to take actions against such as runaway property prices in Taiwan. For many property developers, they would go through the lengths to where the money is, as they would love to nibble away at all the available monetary resources. On some level, it is understandable that people go after where the money is to be independently sufficient, but it would be a different story if they do so in a reckless manner and have no concern for other people being affected by these reckless behaviors. It is not socially responsible, and it is essentially capitalism gone awry. Therefore, we need government to step in, and gain back control through the revision of tax laws.

UNIT 27 實踐夢想、城市發展的成熟化

段落中譯英 ▶ *MP3 027*

　　首先，當世界各地的城市越來越進步發展時，這些城市也因為尋找工作的人不間斷地湧入，而越加壅塞，只因他們想在所謂的「夢想之地」生存、創造屬於自己的生活。換句話說，當城市發展已到如此成熟化的階段，對於想在大城市實踐夢想的年輕人來說，機會將越來越渺茫，而這種城市發展的成熟化，也帶來了其它議題，如城市生活的高開銷等等，所以，對於年輕人來說，尋找代替城市打拼的替代方案來實踐人生理想與目標，是很合理的，並且加上現今科技的發達，回到家鄉打拼儼然是個不錯的選項。

【參考答案】

First of all, as cities around the world are becoming ever more developed, they are also congested with a constant inflow of workers trying to make a living and create a life of their own in these so-called "promise lands." In other words, along with such urban maturation on city development, opportunities can be slimming down for new generations trying to make it in a big city. In addition, there are other issues regarding such maturation, take the high living expenses incurred in big cities for example. Therefore, it would make sense for younger generations to look for the alternative to realize their life vision and goals. Besides, with today's technological advancement, returning back to hometowns can be a great idea.

Part 1 單句中英互譯

Part 2 段落中譯英

Part 3 精選大作文

UNIT 28
核廢料議題、「一擲千金」

　　首先，目前台灣政府面對核能發電廠所衍生的核廢料議題，其措施為將其安排運送至蘭嶼放置。儘管政府已發佈公告，說明類似核廢料這種具放射性的物質，其本身密封的處理方式能夠避免蘭嶼居民的健康受到侵害，但還是無法確切、有效地證明這些居民的健康不會在時間的累積下，受到影響；第二，核能發電廠的建蓋需要一筆可觀的花費，因此，政府在預算花費上一擲千金前，應當多方評估綠能源、再生能源的方案。

_____

_____

_____

_____

_____

_____

【參考答案】

To begin with, the current solution taken by the Taiwanese government to deal with the derivative nuclear wastes is to ship them to the island of Lanyu. Although the government does release a statement ensuring that these radioactive materials are properly enclosed to prevent Lanyu inhabitants from being hazardously affected, there is no certain way to conclude that their health is not impacted in an insidious way. Secondly, the cost of building a nuclear power plant is substantial. The government should be exploring the possibility of greener, more sustainable energy sources before throwing money down the drain on building another plant.

「朱門酒肉臭，路有凍死骨」的社會現象

段落中譯英 ▶ *MP3 029*

　　政府所提出的其中一個解方為社會住宅的推廣方案，讓其能夠造福更多的市民。而儘管社會住宅的申請有相關的法律及規定，但對於年輕世代的許多人來說，社會住宅提供他們一個能夠擁有屬於自己住所的機會，儘管社會住宅的永久所有權並不能夠被購得，而只能以租用的方式使用；因此，我支持政府開始著重社會住宅發展的態度，並支持其將注意力及資金分配到社會住宅方案，因為分配越多，市民越有機會能夠享有基本人權，能夠擁有一個自己的住宅，而能避免勞煩父母、與他們同住。總結來說，我支持政府發展社會住宅的努力、付出，否則這種「朱門酒肉臭，路有凍死骨」的社會現象只會越加嚴重，無法提升一般市民的生活品質。

【參考答案】

One of the solutions proposed by the government is to make social housing more readily available to its citizens. Although there are certain rules and regulations imposed upon social housing applications, for many of the younger generations, the social housing program provides them with a better chance of having a place to call their own, albeit the fact that social housing cannot be permanently owned but is rather dealt with on lease terms. Hence, I support the attention that the development of social housing programs is receiving, because the more attention and funds are allocated towards the programs' development, the more chance that citizens can enjoy what is essentially a basic human right, which is the right to have a house of their own, not the one that parents kindly share with their adult children. All in all, I support the government's effort to promote social housing. Otherwise, the phenomenon of what is described as "The rich get richer, the poor go hungry" will only be getting worse, not able to improve life quality for ordinary citizens.

Part 1 單句中英互譯

Part 2 段落中譯英

Part 3 精選大作文

UNIT 30 反映其價值的薪水、最低法定薪資

段落中譯英 ▶ *MP3 030*

　　首先，台灣的教育體制為台灣的就業市場，每年持續提供高教育程度的研究所、大學畢業生，然而，當與其它已開發國家相比，若以薪水來衡量，台灣對於剛大學畢業的社會新鮮人，其所給予的起薪相對低很多。換句話說，知識份子領取無法反映其價值的薪水，而這社會現象也導致員工對於雇主心生不滿，但正如某管理理論所言，若員工對於所處的工作環境不滿，其生產力及工作品質也將相對地下降，因此，政府應當合理地調高最低法定薪資以提升其工作滿意度。

【參考答案】

For starters, the Taiwanese education system provides a yearly supply of highly-educated batch of postgraduates and college graduates into the workforce. When compared to other developed countries, Taiwan's starting salaries for fresh college graduates are much lower than those of their counterparts in those countries. As a result, higher education graduates are not receiving the kind of salary amount that is an adequate reflection of their educational background. This can further lead to disgruntled work force across the country, and as some management theory indicates, the lesser satisfactory the workforce is with their conditions, the lower productivity and work quality businesses are going to get out of those workers. Therefore, the government should consider reasonably raising the minimum standard upward to increase job satisfaction amongst workers.

UNIT
31

「人多嘴雜」、協調補償金

 段落中譯英 ▶ *MP3 031*

　　如以上所提到的，人多嘴雜容易礙事，尤其當以沒有條理的方式來處理時，將在原本複雜的社會議題上造成更多混亂，比方說，若以城市更新的議題來看，其展現了過度發展的民主政治帶來的優缺點。優點方面，民眾個人能夠有效表達自己的立場，且能在與政府的協商中，盡量維持自己的權益，但反方面來說，城市更新的效率將被拖累、延緩多年，因為政府忙於協商，忙著與民眾協調補償金等議題，而這正是政府過度保護民眾個人權益，忽略了整體社會福祉創造的典型例子。

_____

_____

_____

_____

_____

_____

【參考答案】

As previously stated, too many cooks in the kitchen, if not managed in an organized manner, can easily add more chaos into existing social issues that are already complex in nature. For instance, the issue of urban renewal is a great example showcasing the pros and cons of democracy that is overly developed. For the pros, individuals can have their opinions heard and rights maintained to the fullest if they are unwilling to budge in negotiations with the government. On the flip side of this is that the renewal process can take years if the government is too busy making every individual content with their remuneration. This is a classic example of government overly protecting citizen rights at the expense of realizing the greater good for society.

UNIT 32　利潤最大化為目標、自然資源剝削

段落中譯英　▶ *MP3 032*

　　對於這種作為，我抱持著反對的態度，並且不支持這些大企業背後欲剝削資源的意圖，但卻不願公平合理地對待、回饋受其影響的人民，這樣的作為不僅是不道德的，也是對其所影響的社會不負責任的行為，而純粹以利潤最大化為目標的企業，當地政府應當更加仔細地控管，以維護當地民眾的權益，且當地政府應當注意、認知羊毛出在羊身上的道理，而盡量避免盲目地開放當地的資源，讓大企業以不公平的方式對待當地的政府及民眾。總結而論，我不鼓勵對於開發中國家的勞工及自然資源採取剝削的舉止，而當當地的政府容易短視近利時，應當訂定更多的國際法規及條款，才能杜絕不平等的開發，也才能朝向全球均衡的開發、進步邁進。

【參考答案】

To this practice, I take the opposing stance, and do not support the intent behind these conglomerates who only plan to exploit resources but not intend to fairly reciprocate to those who grab resources from. Such practice is neither ethical nor socially responsible, and those who conduct such business operations purely for the purpose of profit maximization should be more closely regulated to safeguard the rights of the local people. The local governments should be aware of the fact that there is no such thing as a free lunch, and refrain themselves from blindly opening up opportunities for large businesses treating them unfairly. In conclusion, I do not encourage the exploitation of developing countries' workforce and natural resources. As the local governments can be easily blinded by gains in the near future, more international laws and regulations should be enacted to eradicate such unfair practices so that a more balanced development of the world can be made.

UNIT 33

汙染源降到最低、「披荊斬棘」

段落中譯英 ▶ *MP3 033*

　　以我個人的觀點來說，我並不支持此（開發中國家的）論述；首先，今日的商業環境與過去的環境差距甚大，尤其是在工業革命時期的商業環境，更是完全不一樣的，像今日的企業可享有現代科技帶來的便利，而這些便利，對於企業將汙染源降到最低，從任何角度來看，並不會是件很不合理的要求，而且，既然已開發國家已披荊斬棘，克服重重困難建立起環境保護的法規，開發中國家應當好好利用現行法規，畢竟他們最終保護的還是屬於他們自己的自然資源、環境。

_____

_____

_____

_____

_____

_____

【參考答案】

My personal view is that I do not concur with such contention. First of all, today's business climate is much different from the one in the past, certainly not the least different than the one during the Industrial Revolution. Today businesses are blessed with the convenience of modern technology, and with that convenience, keeping the pollution of business operations to the minimum is not too much of an outrageous request by all means. What's more, with the developed countries having blazed a trail for environmental protection, developed countries should take advantage of existing laws and regulations as they are ultimately protecting their own natural resources and environment.

UNIT 34 手機應用程式、「速戰速決」

　　首先，能夠秒連上網際網路的能力，大大地提升人們處理各個生活任務的效率，其中一個例子就是成千上萬已開發的手機應用程式，這些應用程式是用來驅動網路所帶來的效率，將其應用在生活各個領域，舉例來說，銀行業所開發的應用程式，這些程式能夠即時提供帳戶資訊，而這速戰速決的應用，不論是在個人還是企業帳戶上，都可節省處理瑣碎財務事項的時間，而這大幅地改善人們的時間管理，也因此更應當被推廣。

_____

_____

_____

_____

_____

_____

【參考答案】

For starters, being able to connect with the online world in a nanosecond exponentially increases people's efficiency at many tasks. One great example is the myriad of apps that have been invented to better facilitate this efficiency across a wide range of daily life functions. For instance, the apps introduced by the banking industry provide real-time information of a given bank account. This fast and furious way of either personal or business banking saves a lot of people's personal time to deal with frivolous financial matters. This greatly improves how people manage their time, and thus should be promoted.

Part 1 單句中英互譯

Part 2 段落中譯英

Part 3 精選大作文

UNIT 35

「積習成常」、「大打折扣」

 段落中譯英 ▶ *MP3 035*

　　理所當然，人類的行為舉止是積習成常的，這個概念可通用在人們對於新知的認知，及內化吸收的過程，也可運用在人們具體的行為舉止上，而我並不贊同這些「低頭族」的行為，因為我認為他們的行為致使他們錯失生活中許多的美好事物，而這些事物只能透過親身體驗、積極地參與活動，才能有所得，要不然，當活動的參與者一直被智慧型手機上的各種程式打擾時，這些活動所理當帶來的體驗也將大打折扣，舉例來說，在某人與其家族成員的聚會上，若餐桌上的大家時常低頭查看各自手機上的最新訊息，這個聚會也將難以圓滿。

【參考答案】

Granted, humans tend to do things by force of habit. This concept applies to both the ways people perceive and process information, and the physical behaviors of individuals. As for me, I do not view the behaviors of "phubbers" in a favorable light, mainly because I feel that they are missing out on things in life that could only be gained through physical experience. For these certain things in life, individuals need to actively engage in activities. Otherwise, what these activities are supposed to bring to individuals will be greatly diminished when participants are to be continuously interrupted by smartphone uses. For example, one's quality time with family members will not be as pleasurable if those who sit at the dinner table are constantly looking down to check messages on the phone.

UNIT 36　電子商務的蓬勃發展、「無遠弗屆」

 段落中譯英　▶ *MP3 036*

　　為滿足較高層次的需求，其中一個方法是利用電子商務的蓬勃發展，更確切地來說，也就是民眾對於網路購物消費模式的習慣，而當現代人民能夠不愁基本民生問題，比如說不需要擔心下一餐的著落，他們即可開始追尋更高層次需求的滿足，而以網路購物的例子來說，人民所追求的是方便、便利，及其喜愛品牌的優質商品等等，而既然這些需求的演化是自然的進展，我認同網路購物越加受歡迎的趨勢，且相信這蓬勃發展的商業模式，將更提升人民的生活水準，且能夠將進步帶到世界各地，因為電子商務是無遠弗屆的，能夠提供跨洲的服務。

【參考答案】

One way to further facilitate the fulfillment of human needs on higher levels is through the booming development of the E-commerce. More specifically, people's acclimatization to the virtual realm of online shopping. As today's people are well-equipped to throw worries out of the window, worries on basic needs such as whether they are able to pay for the next meal, they are well prepared to pursue the fulfillment of higher needs, and in the case of online shopping, they are going after pursuits such as convenience, choosing quality products with desired brand recognition and so on. Since this is natural progression of human behaviors, I view the trending phenomenon of online shopping in a favorable light, and believe the booming business model could ultimately increase people's living standard even higher and more expansively across the globe, as E-commerce has the capability of providing cross-continent services to customers.

UNIT 37
腦內啡的釋放、「畫地自限」

段落中譯英 ▶ *MP3 037*

　　我個人對此越加盛行的現象抱持著不支持的態度，因為人類自古演化以來，一直都是社交、群居的生物，而科學也證實，我們腦部的先天設計，決定人類生為社交動物的事實，所以，當我們沒有與人面對面交際的機會時，我們的腦部無法接受到適當的刺激及活化，而人類腦部的先天設計，就是鼓勵其多與他人接觸、交際，以刺激腦內啡的釋放，而腦內啡是由人類的中樞系統所釋出，在人類對於痛的阻抗力及快樂的程度上有著正面的影響；另外，多認識人及保有健全的人際關係能為許多人開啟許多機會，且並不只是在工作方面有幫助而已，所以，切勿畫地自限，我們應當多方面嘗試各個機會，而與人見面是達成此目標的好方法之一。

_____

_____

_____

_____

_____

_____

【參考答案】

My personal view on this trending phenomenon is not favorable. As people have been a social creature throughout the evolution of human history, it is scientifically proven that being social with other people is hard-wired in our brain anatomy. When we are not presented with opportunities to be socially engaged in face-to-face scenarios, our brains are not being cerebrally stimulated as they are inherently designed to respond positively to such social stimulations for an adequate amount of endorphins release. Produced by one's central nervous system, endorphins reportedly have the effect of strengthening one's resistance to pain as well as increasing one's level of happiness felt by individuals. Besides, meeting and maintaining strong relationships with people can open many doors to individuals in many ways, not just career-wise. Therefore, as the saying goes, "Go big or go home," we should all try to explore as many opportunities as possible in life, and meeting people is one of the greatest ways to achieve that goal.

UNIT 38
「錙銖必較」、垃圾減量

段落中譯英 ▶ *MP3 038*

　　對於這樣的政策及措施，我個人抱持著支持的態度，因為當人民購買各尺寸的標準垃圾袋須多付費時，政府把握住了大部分人民的心態，那就是盡量減少不必要的開支、增加存款的心態，換句話說，當民眾整體抱持著「錙銖必較」的心態時，政府能夠藉由此措施來成功地減少其人民的垃圾製造量，因人們將開始注意其廢物製造量，以降低他們對於垃圾袋的需求，減少開銷。否則，他們如果不減少垃圾量，就得花更多錢在購買垃圾袋上。

【參考答案】

I personally take a favorable view of this policy and practice. By charging additional fees on people's purchase of standard garbage bags of various sizes, the government takes advantage of people's general mindset to reduce unnecessary costs to increase savings. In other words, as the general public's mentality is mostly what is called "pinching a penny until it screams," the government successfully achieves its goal of reducing garbage amount produced by its countrymen. People will start being mindful of how they can decrease unneeded wastes production in order to consume lesser amount of garbage bags. Otherwise, they will need to spend more money on garbage bags, if they do not curb the amount of their wastes production.

UNIT 39 「一分耕耘，一分收穫」、「前人種樹，後人乘涼」

段落中譯英 ▶ *MP3 039*

　　然而，儘管大眾運輸系統能夠帶來許多的便利，其計畫及建造的過程通常會花上許多的時間及政府的可用資源，也因為這樣，有些人會質疑建造、擴建此系統的需要性，我個人則是支持政府將時間及資源用在此系統的建造上，儘管會對現在的居民造成一時的不便，並會花上許多資源，但就像諺語說的：「一分耕耘，一分收穫」，這也是人生中不變的道理。這項投資可本質上視成是，以前人種樹，後人乘涼之姿，為後代考量利益。

【參考答案】

However, as much as many benefits that a public transit system is capable of bringing, the planning and construction process can take an incredible amount of time and consume many available resources from the government. As a result, some are skeptical of the necessity of building and expanding such a transit system. I personally support the time and efforts that a government is committing to constructing the system, despite the temporary inconvenience and the large amount of invested resources. This kind of upfront investment is necessary as the saying goes, "no pains, no gains." The investment can essentially be viewed as planting pears for your heirs.

UNIT 40

黑心企業、「繩之以法」

　　我個人的觀點認為，某些食品產業的不肖商人願意犧牲民眾的健康，以換取較大的利潤，是很可恥的行為，而商人這種昧心取利，以獲得不法利潤的行為，應當被社會唾棄、鄙視。然而，社會大眾對於這些黑心企業所採取的抵制行為，影響力也是有限，因此，政府應當介入，制訂較嚴謹的法律條文，以防企業再度鑽法律漏洞、昧心取利，確保民眾權益，使其能夠享有安全，且對健康有益的食品。總結來說，我認為政府應當適時介入，以將這些黑心企業繩之以法。要不然，這些黑心的行為無法有效地被制止，未來也將有更多商人仿效、昧心取利地追求財富。

【參考答案】

Personally, I find the behavior despicable because certain businessmen in the food industry can so willingly disregard people's health conditions only to achieve greater margins of profit on their companies' products. The profits earned this way are indeed ill-gotten gains, which should be looked down upon by the whole society. However, there is not much the general public can do to try to boycott against these unethical companies' products. Rather, the real power lies in the government's hand to pass stringent laws to avoid businesses earning filthy lucre through legal loopholes again, and to protect people's rights to safe, health-beneficial food products. In conclusion, I think the government should step in to legally hold those who conduct unethical businesses accountable. Otherwise, this kind of behavior will not be effectively stopped, and more businessmen would also engage in the pursuit of filthy lucre in the future.

UNIT 41 淨化水源、「近水惜水」

 段落中譯英 ▶ *MP3 041*

　　我個人支持許多的公益團體，為了解決非洲大陸水資源危機而做的努力將乾淨安全的飲用水帶到非洲各個角落裡。而在這些的努力、嘗試中，現代科學家也帶來了許多的突破，他們發明了許多簡易好用、低成本的裝置，來幫助人民方便地享用可飲用水資源，而其中一項裝置是名為「生命飲管」的產品，它能夠過濾、淨化不乾淨的水源至乾淨、可飲用的狀態，這麼一來，充滿汙染物及細菌的水源將能夠藉由「生命飲管」，在幾秒鐘內簡易地淨化為可飲用的水源。綜合上述，已開發國家的人民，應當珍惜其生活中唾手可得的飲用水資源，並且體現「近水惜水」的精神。

【參考答案】

To solve this water crisis in Africa, I personally support many charitable organizations' efforts to bring clean, safe drinkable water to every corner of the continent. Among these efforts, there are a few breakthroughs made by modern scientists to bring easy-to-use, low-cost apparatuses to those who otherwise do not have easy access to clean drinking water. One of these tools is the product named "LifeStraw," which has the capability to filter and purify water from unclean sources to clean, drinkable state. This way, water with pollutants and harmful bacteria can be easily cleansed through "LifeStraw," and thus available for drinking in a matter of seconds. With the above said, those who are lucky enough to live in developed countries should cherish drinkable water resources that are readily available in their lives.

UNIT 42
「不遺餘力」、城市的規劃及發展

段落中譯英 ▶ *MP3 042*

　　當空汙是如此嚴重的議題時，台灣的政府也不遺餘力，直接面對這個問題。而我也支持台灣政府，其嘗試將這個國家的都市區域，朝向綠化的方向發展的努力，就拿台北市來說，台北的空氣污染程度，跟十年前相比，已大幅度地降低，而現今的路旁也規劃種植了許多的植物及樹木，目的就是將綠化的空間能夠成功融入城市的規劃及發展，並且，有許多廢棄區域被活化，轉化為公開的大眾綠色空間，不只提供了民眾休閒的安全去處，也使得光合作用的運行足以抵抗導因於空氣污染而產生的有害元素。

【參考答案】

With air pollution being such a serious issue, the Taiwanese government is tackling the issue of air pollution head on. I support the government's conscious efforts to make some of the country's urban areas greener with clean air, take the capital city of Taipei for example. In Taipei, the level of air pollution has been effectively reduced in comparison to the quality of air decades ago. There are much more plants and trees being planted along the streets to purposefully integrate more greenery into the city's urban development. There are countless examples of deserted areas being rejuvenated and transformed into open public green space that not only provides a safe place for people to hang out, but also enables the interaction of the photosynthesis to counter with harmful elements resulting from air pollution.

UNIT
43
擴展財富、掠奪資源

　　首先，我們須瞭解，人類在工業革命時期的當下，並不瞭解掠奪地球資源的潛藏後果，所以在當下，大部分人都以自己的利益為重，積極地擴展財富，而當時許多的工廠主人，時常為了更多的利潤及擴張，而不擇手段、貪得無厭。當然，人類現在已無法再以無知為後盾，因為我們已知若我們繼續以莽撞的行為，並且以自我為中心的心態來掠奪資源的話，是要付出代價的。要幫助降低土壤汙染的話，我們可從降低生活中不必要的浪費、不使用塑膠袋、避免買瓶裝礦泉水，純喝淨化的自來水等行為開始著手，都可有效幫助降低土壤的汙染。

【參考答案】

Firstly, in the period of the Industrial Revolution, people were not so educated on the potential effect of them exploiting the planet for resources. At the time, people were mostly looking out for themselves, aggressively going after ways to expand their wealth. Back then, greedy factory owners would sell their own mothers for substantial profits and more expansion. Nevertheless, ignorance is no longer an excuse for humankind, as we have come to realize the fact that there will be consequences if we just recklessly grab resources as we please. Some examples that we can help decrease soil contamination are to reduce unnecessary wastes in our daily lives, not to use plastic bags, not to purchase bottled water but just simply purified tap water for drinking, and so on.

Part 1 單句中英互譯

Part 2 段落中譯英

Part 3 精選大作文

UNIT 44

漁業捕撈、「自生自滅」

 段落中譯英迹 ▶ *MP3 044*

　　這些殘酷、不人道的漁業捕撈現象，其中一個例子就是對於鯊魚的迫害。在某些地區，人們捕抓鯊魚，並當場將鰭割下，因為這些鰭是鯊魚身上最獲利的部位，但更糟的是，這些鯊魚之後就被丟回深海裡，這實在可說是人類對於其他生物剝削手段的極致案例之一了，因為這些失去鰭的鯊魚，也失去了牠們在其原本棲息的深海裡生存的能力，所以本質上來說，牠們根本就是被棄置在深海裡自生自滅、等待死亡；若要有效地杜絕這類對海底生物的剝削手段，政府及國際組織應當同心協力，一同防止漁業過度捕撈的現象再度發生。

_____

_____

_____

_____

_____

_____

【參考答案】

One of these cruel and inhumane practices employed by some in the fishing industry includes the treatment of sharks. In certain regions, sharks are caught and their fins are cut off on the spot. What's worse, as the fins are the most valuable part on the body of sharks, many of those sharks are tossed right back into the deep sea. This is probably one of the purest forms of exploitation on these creatures as the sharks are essentially left to die when stripped of fins in the sea, unable to swim. To effectively bring this kind of exploitation to an end, governments and international organizations should work together to prevent overfishing from happening ever again.

UNIT 45 醫美整型手術、施打肉毒桿菌

今日手術科技的進步，讓人們能夠享有更安全的醫美整型手術，甚至有無痛手術的選項，而其降低的手術疼痛感，以及更快速的術後復元期間，讓人們對於醫美的需求量大增。舉例來說，在美國有許多人，包括年紀在三十區間的輕熟年齡層，都很風行藉由肉毒桿菌來維持外貌，並且認為年輕時定期地施打肉毒桿菌，能夠有效延緩外表的老化。整體來說，我支持人們藉由醫美整型來提升自我信心，只要符合以安全為前提的原則。但另一方面來說，正如成語「名不符實」所形容的，人們應當也要以積極的態度，在內在美的提升上下功夫。

【參考答案】

With today's surgical improvement, people have access to a much safer choice of surgical procedures. Nowadays, some surgical techniques even make the idea of painless operations possible. This reduced pain, coupled with the improved, shortened recovery time, boosts people's interests in resorting to cosmetic surgeries for their preferred looks. For example, it is very popular for people, even those at a relatively younger ages such as their mid-thirties, to go for Botox injections in the United States. For those young people who go for shots of Botox on a regular basis, they believe such injections will yield some sort of preventative effects. Essentially, they believe that receiving regular shots of Botox at a younger age can ultimately slow the pace of aging on their looks. In general, I support people's efforts to increase their level of confidence through plastic surgeries, but only on the premise of ensured safety. On the other hand, as the saying goes, "All that glitters is not gold." People need to also work on their inner beauty as much as on their outer one.

UNIT 46　「謀事在人，成事在天」、「雙刃劍」

　　換句話說，今日的癌症病患，正如「謀事在人，成事在天」所說，必須學會如何接受，並不輕易放棄，堅強、持續與病魔奮鬥。以現有各式各樣的癌症治療法來說，化療也許是治療上最常見的，而其療效也常被認為具有所謂的「雙刃劍」效果，因為化療不只毀滅癌症細胞，同一時間也對正常、良性的細胞造成衝擊，而因為有太多這些無法控制的變因，癌症病患有時會因療程的不確定性感到氣餒，進而對治療感到憂鬱、悲觀。

【參考答案】

In other words, Today's cancer patients have to come to terms with the fact that all they can do is to remain positive and do not stop fighting, just as the saying "man proposes, God disposes" goes. In terms of cancer treatments that are currently available, there are a variety of options. Among these options, chemotherapy is probably the most common one in practice, and this therapy is often considered to be the sort of double edged sword treatment where not only cancer cells are destroyed through the treatment, but also the normal, good ones. Because of the fact that too many uncontrollable variables at stake, cancer patients can sometimes be discouraged by the uncertainty of the treatment and eventually become depressed and pessimistic.

收錄「高分範文」並錄音，方便考生通勤時反覆聽誦，增加語感和答題實力。請務必在觀看答案前，先觀看作文題目後再提筆於時限內完成作文，於之後再對照範文比較，欲考取高分的考生也務必要達到等同範文等級的佳作。

PART 3

UNIT
01

畫面過於聳動 ── 搭配電影：
《獨家腥聞》（Nightcrawler）

WRITING TASK 2

TOPIC

"The media today present too many provocative images; instead, the media should place more emphasis on the deeper meaning behind those images." Do you agree or disagree with the statement? Use specific details and examples to support your viewpoint.

「當今的媒體呈現太多聳動的畫面；反之，媒體應該放更多重心去探討那些畫面背後的深層意義。」你同意或不同意以上敘述？請使用精準的細節和例證支持你的論點。

 **單句中譯英**

❶ 然而，我認為在民主社會有限的媒體審查制度之下，深入探討畫面背後的觀念並不是媒體的責任，而且聳動的畫面只是顯示媒體蓬勃的競爭現象。

_____

【參考答案】

However, I concede that in a democratic society with limited censorship of the media, it is rarely the duty of the media to probe further into the concepts behind those images, and that provocative images are simply indicative of the vibrant competitions in the media.

❷ 此外，隨著網路問世，媒體資源已呈爆炸性的發展，導致可能是媒體史上最激烈的競爭狀態。

_____

_____

【參考答案】

Besides, with the advent of the Internet, there has been an explosion of media resources, which leads to probably the fiercest competition in media history.

❸ 因此，呈現聳動的畫面已演變成打動消費者最快速的方式，雖然偶爾道德方面的問題會被提出來。

_____

_____

【參考答案】

Therefore, presenting provocative images has evolved into one of the fastest ways to reach consumers, though occasionally ethical questions are raised.

❹ 暫時忽略道德議題的話，運用聳動的畫面只是個高效率的行銷策略。

_____

_____

【參考答案】

If ethical issues are disregarded, utilizing sensational images is merely an efficient marketing strategy.

❺ 此外，這種畫面的構成元素是高度可議的，因為不同的人對這些畫面抱持的標準有所差異。

_____

_____

【參考答案】

Moreover, what constitutes such images is highly disputable, as various people hold divergent standards for them.

高分範文搶先看　▶ MP3 047

Upon first glance, the statement seems like a **justifiable** critique, considering there's so much violence and **risqué** content in the media nowadays. However, I concede that in a **democratic** society with limited **censorship** of the media, it is rarely the duty of the media to probe further into the concepts behind those images, and that **provocative** images are simply indicative of the **vibrant** competitions in the media.

First, all companies are pursuing the utmost profit, and those in the media are no exception. Besides, with the advent of the Internet, there has been an **explosion** of media resources, which leads to probably the fiercest competition in media history. Therefore, presenting **provocative** images has evolved into one of the

乍看之下，敘述似乎是句正當的批評，考慮到當今媒體充斥著暴力和幾近傷風敗俗的內容。然而，我認為在民主社會有限的媒體審查制度之下，深入探討畫面背後的觀念並不是媒體的責任，而且聳動的畫面只是顯示媒體蓬勃的競爭現象。

首先，所有的公司都在追求最高利潤，媒體業也不例外。此外，隨著網路問世，媒體資源已呈爆炸性的發展，導致可能是媒體史上最激烈的競爭狀態。因此，呈現聳動的畫面已演變成打動消費者最快速的方式，雖然偶爾道德方面的問題會被提出來。例如，廣告常常運

fastest ways to reach consumers, though occasionally ethical questions are raised. For instance, **advertisements** often apply **piquant** images to draw spectators' attention. By the same token, news programs have no choice but to flow with the tide to **boost** ratings, and **tabloids** have to publish **spine-tingling** photos to increase sales. If ethical issues are **disregarded**, utilizing **sensational** images is merely an efficient marketing strategy.

Moreover, what **constitutes** such images is highly disputable, as various people hold **divergent** standards for them. I would argue that it is not the media's responsibility to provide deeper concepts. On the contrary, it is the viewers' responsibility to research further should they be interested. For example, as tabloids and melodrama **abound**,

用辛辣刺激的畫面去吸引觀眾的注意。同理，新聞節目不得不隨波逐流地跟上這股趨勢，以提高收視率，而八卦媒體必須出版令人血脈噴張的照片，以提升銷售量。暫時忽略道德議題的話，運用聳動的畫面只是個高效率的行銷策略。

而且，這種畫面的構成元素是高度可議的，因為不同的人對這些畫面抱持的標準有所差異。我主張提供更深層的觀念並不是媒體的責任。相反地，做出更深入的探討應該是觀眾的責任，萬一他們有興趣的話。例如，雖然八卦媒體和煽情戲劇節目到處充斥，如果觀眾想要獲取知識性的內容，他們可以轉向公共電視或教育

audiences can turn to public television and education **channels** if they wish to have access to **intellectual** discourse. In other words, it is not mandatory for the media to emphasize **profound** meaning.

In conclusion, I disagree with the statement because it **undermines** the diversity of the media. It is not the media's job to **instill** concepts into us; rather, it is the viewers' job to search for meaning.

頻道。也就是說，不須強制媒體去強調深層意義。

　　總而言之，我不同意題目敘述，因為它輕忽了媒體的多樣性。灌輸觀念給我們並不是媒體的工作，反之，追尋意義應該是觀眾的工作。

UNIT 02

藉由電影學習外國事物 — 搭配電影：《三個傻瓜》（3 Idiots）

 WRITING TASK 2

TOPIC

"Movies tell us a lot about the country where they were produced. Name a movie and explain what you have learned about the country by watching it." Use specific details and examples to support your choice.

「電影透露出電影製作國家的很多事物。指出一部電影，並闡述你從那部電影學到關於其國家的哪些事物。」請使用精準的細節和例證支持你的選擇。

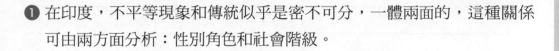

單句中譯英

❶ 在印度，不平等現象和傳統似乎是密不可分，一體兩面的，這種關係可由兩方面分析：性別角色和社會階級。

【參考答案】

Inequality and traditions seem to be intertwined in India as two sides of the same coin, which can be analyzed in two aspects: gender roles and social hierarchy.

❷ 首先，關於性別角色，電影強調兩性都背負著傳統期待。

【參考答案】

First, regarding gender roles, the movie emphasizes that males and females carry conventional expectations.

❸ 兒子必須追求能保障他們高聲望工作的學位，而女兒必須藉由跟富人結婚為家庭帶來榮耀。

【參考答案】

Sons must pursue degrees that guarantee them prestigious jobs, while daughters must honor their parents by marrying richer men.

❹ 然而，女性比男性面對更多不平等。如同電影裡一位醫學系女學生暗示的，當面對婚姻，家族名譽比女性個人意志重要多了。

_____

_____

【參考答案】

However, women face more inequality than men, as a female medical student in the film suggests that when it comes to marriage, family honor precedes a woman's individuality.

❺ 不過，年輕世代對傳統的抵抗是有希望的，如同男性角色堅持追求夢想，女性角色逃離她自己的婚禮。

_____

_____

【參考答案】

Nonetheless, there is hope for the younger generation's defiance against tradition, as the male characters insist on pursuing their dreams, and the female character flees from her own wedding.

高分範文搶先看　▶ MP3 048

Movies certainly enlighten us in many ways, broadening our horizon and allowing us to learn about countries we have never been to. I would draw on the movie, "3 Idiots", to explain what I learned about current Indian society, particularly about inequality and the clash between traditions and new thoughts.

Inequality and traditions seem to be **intertwined** in India as two sides of the same coin, which can be analyzed in two aspects: gender roles and social **hierarchy**. First, regarding gender roles, the movie emphasizes that males and females carry **conventional** expectations. Sons must pursue degrees that guarantee them **prestigious** jobs, while daughters must honor their parents by marrying richer men. For instance,

電影的確在很多方面啟發我們，拓展我們的視野，並讓我們學到關於未曾造訪的國家的事物。我將引用《三個傻瓜》這部電影闡述我從這部電影學到關於現代印度社會的某些現象，尤其是不平等現象及傳統與新思維的衝突。

在印度，不平等現象和傳統似乎是密不可分，一體兩面的，這種關係可由兩方面分析：性別角色和社會階級。首先，關於性別角色，電影強調兩性都背負著傳統期待。兒子必須追求能保障他們高聲望工作的學位，而女兒必須藉由跟富人結婚為家庭帶來榮耀。例如，三個主要男性角色裡，有兩位是因為父母的期待，才研讀工程學。然而，女性比男性面

two of the three major male characters study Engineering because of their parents' expectations. However, women face more **inequality** than men, as a female medical student in the film suggests that when it comes to marriage, family honor **precedes** a woman's individuality. Nonetheless, there is hope for the younger generation's **defiance** against tradition, as the male characters insist on pursuing their dreams, and the female character flees from her own wedding.

Secondly, traditional social **hierarchy**, namely the caste system, still exerts enormous influence, as suggested by the story of the **protagonist**, Rancho, who **conceals** his true identity as an orphaned servant and is hired by his employer to acquire a degree in his son's name. Despite

對更多不平等。如同電影裡一位醫學系女學生暗示的,當面對婚姻,家族名譽比女性個人意志重要多了。不過,年輕世代對傳統的抵抗是有希望的,如同男性角色堅持追求夢想,女性角色逃離她自己的婚禮。

第二,傳統社會階級,即種姓制度,仍發揮極大的影響力。由主角藍丘的故事可略知一二。他隱瞞真實的身分—失怙的僕人,被老闆僱用以他兒子的名義去取得學位。儘管花了四年取得學位,他無法以自己的真名宣稱擁有這文憑。幸運的是,藍丘的快樂結局教導

having devoted years to attain the degree, he cannot claim the degree under his real name. Fortunately, the happy ending for Rancho teaches us that the **underprivileged** can turn the tables by utilizing their knowledge.

Undeniably, traditions might be difficult to break, but the contemporary Indian society is changing. The movie conveys an important message that the younger generation in India can indeed break the **shackles** of traditions.

我們處於社會劣勢的人，利用知識仍有可能翻轉命運。

不可否認地，傳統可能很難破除，但現代印度社會正在改變。這部電影傳達一則重要的訊息，印度的年輕世代的確有可能打破傳統的枷鎖。

UNIT 03

偏好電影還是小說 ─ 搭配電影:《科學怪人》(Frankenstein) 與《瘋狂麥斯》(Mad Max)

 WRITING TASK 2

TOPIC

"Some people prefer watching movies, while others prefer reading novels. Which do you prefer?" Explain the reasons for your preference with specific examples and details.

「有些人偏好看電影,而有些人偏好讀小說。你偏好哪一個?」請使用精確的細節和例證解釋你偏好的理由。

單句中譯英

❶ 支持我的偏好的第一個理由是，小說裡的元素常常被作者的背景限制，然而電影能融入當代觀點和豐富的文化面向，使電影對觀眾而言更容易理解。

_____

_____

【參考答案】

The first reason for my preference is that elements in fiction are often limited by the writer's background, while movies incorporate contemporary viewpoints and various cultural dimensions, making them more approachable to the audience.

❷ 同樣地，讀者對小說的理解能力也會受限於個人背景，但看電影可以拓展理解能力。

_____

_____

【參考答案】

Likewise, the readers' comprehension of a novel is confined by their personal background, which can be broadened by watching movies.

❸ 例如，一位從未讀過英國文學的讀者在想像珍‧奧斯汀小說裡的生活風格及歷史背景時，可能會遭遇困難。

_____

_____

【參考答案】

For instance, a reader who has never studied British literature would have difficulty visualizing the lifestyles and historical background in Jane Austen's novels.

❹ 但是，藉由觀賞小說改編成的電影，他能立刻理解那些元素。

_____

_____

【參考答案】

However, by watching movie adaptations, he can perceive those elements instantly.

❺ 另一個例子是 19 世紀的科幻小說，例如《科學怪人》和《時光機器》，內含了超越作者那個時代的非凡視野。

_____

_____

【參考答案】

Another example is that sci-fi novels, such as _Frankenstein_ and _The Time Machine_, written in the 19th century encompass extraordinary vision far ahead of the authors' time.

高分範文搶先看　▶ MP3 049

Both movies and novels have distinctive advantages. I prefer movies to novels because of the diversity of angles and technologies in movies.

The first reason for my preference is that elements in fiction are often limited by the writer's background, while movies incorporate contemporary viewpoints and various cultural dimensions, making them more **approachable** to the audience. Likewise, the readers' **comprehension** of a novel is confined by their personal background, which can be broadened by watching movies. For instance, a reader who has never studied British literature would have difficulty **visualizing** the lifestyles and historical background in Jane Austen's

電影及小說都有各自獨特的優點。我偏好電影多於小說，理由是電影裡多樣化的角度和科技。

支持我的偏好的第一個理由是，小說裡的元素常常被作者的背景限制，然而電影能融入當代觀點和豐富的文化面向，使電影對觀眾而言更容易理解。同樣地，讀者對小說的理解能力也會受限於個人背景，但看電影可以拓展理解能力。例如，一位從未讀過英國文學的讀者在想像珍・奧斯汀小說裡的生活風格及歷史背景時，可能會遭遇困難。但是，藉由觀賞小說改編成的電影，他能立刻理解那些元素。另一個例子是 19 世紀的科幻小說，例如《科學怪人》和《時光機器》，內含了超越

novels. However, by watching movie adaptations, he can **perceive** those elements instantly. Another example is that sci-fi novels, such as *Frankenstein* and *The Time Machine*, written in the 19th century **encompass extraordinary** vision far ahead of the authors' time. Yet, movie adaptations of those novels in the 21st century can provide more diverse angles by integrating new technologies and new scientific theories.

The second reason concerns the advancement of technology. While the **genres** of novels have not evolved dramatically over the past few centuries, movie technologies have gone through enormous **amelioration** in merely one century. With the advancement of 4DX technology, fictional elements are materialized in theaters, which

作者那個時代的非凡視野。然而，在 21 世紀，改編自那些小說的電影能藉由融入新科技和新科學理論，提供更豐富的角度。

第二個理由是關於科技的發達。小說的類型在過去幾個世紀沒有太明顯的演進，相對而言，電影科技僅在一個世紀內就經歷了巨大的進步。隨著 4DX 科技的進步，虛構的元素能在電影院裡被具體化，這是讀小說不可能辦到的。現在我們可以沉浸在類似電影角色經歷的感官體驗中。想像一下讀《瘋狂麥斯》的小說和在 4DX

cannot be achieved by reading novels. We can now **immerse** ourselves in similar sensations to those movie characters experience. Imagine the **discrepancy** between reading the **novelization** "Mad Max" and watching it in a 4DX theater where we can feel the seats vibrating, wind blowing, and mist sprayed on us; contrarily, reading the **novelization** is **sedentary**.

In sum, movies bridge viewers from different backgrounds and add current **perspectives**, without requiring viewers to possess any relevant knowledge, as well as create more thrills with technologies, which explains my **propensity** to choose movies over novels.

戲院觀賞這部電影的差別,在戲院裡,我們能感受到椅子震動,風吹拂著,及霧氣對著我們噴灑;相反地,讀小説是靜止不動的。

總而言之,電影縮短不同背景的觀眾間的距離,並加入當代觀點,不需要觀眾擁有相關知識,而且能運用科技創造更多刺激,以上解釋了為何我傾向偏好電影多於小說。

UNIT 04

大學教育在於培養價值觀，而不是為工作做準備 — 搭配電影：《蒙娜麗莎的微笑》（Mona Lisa Smile）

 WRITING TASK 2

TOPIC

"The purpose of university education is to help students form a set of values, not to prepare them for future jobs". Do you agree or disagree with the statement? Use specific details and examples to support your viewpoint.

「大學教育的目的是幫助學生建構價值觀，不是讓他們對未來的工作做準備。」你同意或不同意以上敘述？請使用精準的細節和例證支持你的論點。

🎓 單句中譯英

❶ 在大部份的西方國家，職訓學院和大學之間有明顯的區別。

_____

_____

【參考答案】

In most western countries, there is a clear distinction between vocational colleges and universities.

❷ 如果有人認為他教育投資的目的只是找到工作，念職訓學院似乎是比較明智的選擇。

_____

_____

【參考答案】

If one considers that his investment in education will solely lead to landing a job, studying in a vocational college seems a wiser choice.

❸ 畢竟，職訓學院的核心功能是讓學生準備好實用技能以因應市場需求。

_____

_____

【參考答案】

After all, the core function of vocational colleges is to equip students with practical skills to meet market demands.

❹ 相反地，大學是由各式各樣的科系組合而成，包括各種科學和人文科系，也就意謂著學術環境提供的是文化及跨學科的交流；藉由這些交流，教授傳授他們的智慧，而學生能吸收這些智慧以協助發展自我的價值觀。

_____

_____

【參考答案】

On the contrary, universities are constituted by diversified departments, from sciences to humanities, indicating that the academic environment provides cultural and interdisciplinary dialogues from which professors impart their wisdom which students can imbibe to help develop personal values.

❺ 此外，大學教育應該賦予我們運用個人價值觀掌控人生方向的能力。

_____

_____

【參考答案】

Furthermore, university education should enable us to steer our lives with personal values.

高分範文搶先看　▶ MP3 050

Although the global recession has made most people feel that the purpose of university education should be to prepare students for jobs, I am **inclined** to agree with the statement.

My major argument concerns the core functions of different educational institutions. In most western countries, there is a clear **distinction** between vocational colleges and universities. If one considers that his **investment** in education will solely lead to landing a job, studying in a vocational college seems a wiser choice. After all, the core function of **vocational** colleges is to equip students with practical skills to meet market demands. On the contrary, universities are **constituted** by diversified departments, from sciences to

雖然全球經濟萎縮讓大部份人覺得大學教育的目的應該是使學生對工作做好準備，我仍傾向同意題目的敘述。

我的主要論點是關於不同教育機構的核心功能。在大部份的西方國家，職訓學院和大學之間有明顯的區別。如果有人認為他教育投資的目的只是找到工作，念職訓學院似乎是比較明智的選擇。畢竟，職訓學院的核心功能是讓學生準備好實用技能以因應市場需求。相反地，大學是由各式各樣的科系組合而成，包括各種科學和人文科系，也就意謂著學術環境提供的是文化及跨學科的交流；藉由這些交流，教授傳授他們的智慧，而學生能吸收這些智慧以協助發

humanities, indicating that the academic environment provides cultural and **interdisciplinary** dialogues from which professors **impart** their wisdom which students can **imbibe** to help develop personal values.

Furthermore, university education should enable us to **steer** our lives with personal values. Take two characters in the movie, Mona Lisa Smile , for example. One student followed **mainstream** expectations to be come a housewife, an ideal "job" for women in the 1950s; on the other hand, another student gave up the opportunity to study in law school, choosing to be a housewife over being a lawyer. Conforming to the mainstream left the former feeling **enslaved** in her marriage, while choosing her family over being a lawyer left the latter feeling fulfilled

展自我的價值觀。

此外，大學教育應該賦予我們運用個人價值觀掌控人生方向的能力。以電影《蒙娜麗莎的微笑》的兩個角色為例，一位學生遵守主流價值，成為家庭主婦，這是 1950 年代女性的最佳「工作」；另一方面，另一位學生放棄讀法學院的機會，選擇當家庭主婦，而不是律師。遵守主流價值觀使得前者在婚姻中感到被奴役，而選擇家庭讓後者感到圓滿，因為她依循的是自我的價值觀。不管我們選擇什麼工作，個人價值觀能作為有意義的生活的精神支柱。這就是為何大學應該協助學生建構價值觀。

because she followed her own value system. No matter what jobs we choose, our individual values serve as an **anchor** for a meaningful life, which is why universities should assist students to construct value systems.

While the two purposes mentioned in the statement are not mutually **exclusive**, I stand firm behind my stance that the ultimate goal of universities lies in helping students cultivate individual values, without which life is without anchor, regardless of our jobs.

題目敘述提及的兩種目的並非彼此衝突，但我仍堅持我的立場，大學的終極目標是協助學生培養個人價值觀，沒有個人價值觀的人生是沒有精神支柱的，不管我們的工作為何。

UNIT 05

年輕人是否能教導長輩 — 搭配名人故事史蒂夫・賈伯斯（Steve Jobs）及馬克・祖客柏（Mark Zuckerberg）

WRITING TASK 2

TOPIC

"Young people can hardly teach anything to older people." Do you agree or disagree with the statement? Use specific details and examples to support your standpoint.

「年輕人幾乎不能教長輩任何事。」你同意或不同意以上敘述？請使用精準的細節和例證支持你的論點。

單句中譯英

❶ 然而，鑒於現今社會變遷的快速步調及經濟波動，兩個世代的社會背景不盡相似。

_____

_____

【參考答案】

However, the social backgrounds of two generations are rarely similar, considering the fast pace of social changes and economic fluctuations nowadays.

❷ 因此，年長者引用自身經驗教導年輕人的觀念是高度可議的。

_____

_____

【參考答案】

Hence, the notion of older ones teaching younger ones by drawing on personal experiences is highly controvertible.

❸ 事實上，面對第三次工業革命，即製造業的數位化，所影響的全球變遷，成長時已熟悉電腦科技的年輕人能教導年長者更多事物。

_____

_____

【參考答案】

In fact, faced with the global vicissitudes influenced by the third Industrial Revolution, i.e., the digitalization of manufacturing, younger ones who grew up familiarizing themselves with computer technologies have much more to teach older ones.

④ 兩個明顯的例證能支持我的立場，蘋果電腦創辦人史帝夫．賈伯斯和臉書創辦人馬克．祖克柏。

_____

_____

【參考答案】

To support my stance, two pronounced examples are illustrated, Steve Jobs, the founder of Apple Computers and Mark Zuckerberg, Facebook founder.

⑤ 賈伯斯在他二十歲初頭就有個信念，要創造每個人都能擁有的電腦。

_____

_____

【參考答案】

Jobs' belief in creating a computer for everyone arose in his early twenties.

高分範文搶先看　▶ MP3 051

Although the statement that the young can teach little to the old sounds **ostensibly** plausible, I hold a contrary stance in light of the **fallacious** reasoning for the statement and obvious examples that refute such an assertion.

The reason for my disagreement is that the claim is based on a **conspicuous fallacy**, that is, the "all things are equal" fallacy, meaning situations remain the same in different places and times. However, the social backgrounds of two generations are rarely similar, considering the fast pace of social changes and economic **fluctuations** nowadays; hence, the **notion** of older ones teaching younger ones by drawing on personal experiences is highly **controvertible**. In fact, faced with the global **vicissitudes** influenced

雖然年輕人幾乎無法教導長輩這句話貌似合理，我持反對立場，因為此敘述是依據邏輯謬誤而成立，並有明顯的例子能反駁此敘述。

我不同意此敘述的原因是因為此敘述根據的是一個明顯的邏輯謬誤，即「一切皆同」的謬誤，指的是在不同的地方和時代，情況都相同。然而，鑒於現今社會變遷的快速步調及經濟波動，兩個世代的社會背景不盡相似。因此，年長者引用自身經驗教導年輕人的觀念是高度可議的。事實上，面對第三次工業革命，即製造業的數位化，所影響的全球變遷，成長時已熟悉電腦科技的年輕人能教導年長者更多事物。

by the third Industrial Revolution, i.e., the **digitalization** of manufacturing, younger ones who grew up familiarizing themselves with computer technologies have much more to teach older ones.

To support my stance, two **pronounced** examples are illustrated, Steve Jobs, the founder of Apple Computers and Mark Zuckerberg, Facebook founder. Jobs' belief in creating a computer for everyone arose in his early twenties. Jobs demonstrated to his senior business partners that not only could his vision be realized, but also design and **practicability** could be **integrated**. Zuckerberg also **initiated** his business in his twenties. Like Jobs, Zuckerberg thinks **unconventionally**. There had been social networks for university students before

兩個明顯的例證能支持我的立場，蘋果電腦創辦人史帝夫・賈伯斯和臉書創辦人馬克・祖克柏。賈伯斯在他二十歲初頭就有個信念，要創造每個人都能擁有的電腦。賈伯斯向年長的事業夥伴證明不但他的遠見成真，設計和實用性也能被整合。祖克柏也在二十多歲時開創他的事業。就像賈伯斯，祖克柏以非傳統的方式思考。在臉書之前，已經有給大學生使用的社交網絡，但是他看到機會並將那些網站轉變成大眾的社交網路。賈伯斯和祖克柏都抓住年長者沒看到的機會，這的確是值得學習的。

Facebook, yet he spotted the opportunity of turning those into a social network for the public. Both Jobs and Zuckerberg seized opportunities that older people did not see, which certainly offers a lesson to learn.

Confronted with dramatic global changes, old people have much to learn from young ones as the latter are living through those changes, thus more capable of offering insights.

面對劇烈的全球變化，年長者能從年輕人身上學習很多，因為年輕人正親身經歷那些變化，因此更能提供相關洞見。

UNIT 06

從人生中學習：聽取建議或親身經驗 — 搭配電影《心靈捕手》（Good Will Hunting）

 WRITING TASK 2

TOPIC

"Some people learn about life by listening to the suggestions of elders or friends, while others learn about life through personal experience". Compare the advantages of these two ways and state your preference. Use specific details and examples to support your preference.

「有些人藉由聽從長輩或朋友的建議學習關於人生的事物，而其他人透過親自體驗學習人生。」請比較兩種方式的優點並提出你偏好哪一種。使用精準的細節和例證支持你的偏好。

單句中譯英

❶ 我傾向認為在少年期之前，如果多聽從他人建議，探索世界的過程會比較順利，然而當一個人成為年輕成人，透過親自體驗會比較有益處。

【參考答案】

I am inclined to hold the opinion that before one enters adolescence, he would explore the world more smoothly if given more advice from others, yet as one becomes a young adult, it is more beneficial to learn through personal experience.

❷ 首先，不難理解的是從我們的自我意識在嬰兒期晚期萌芽，到兒童期晚期個人身份開始形成這段期間，我們不但依賴長輩，也依賴同儕的建議，為的是生理和心理方面都能正常發展。

【參考答案】

First, it is easily comprehensible that from the moment our sense of self initially emerges in late infancy to the moment we begin forming our individual identity in late childhood, we rely on advice from not only elders but also our peers in order to develop normally both physical and mental.

❸ 生理上，小孩有原始的本能要依附照顧者，為了生存而尋求關於生活基本面的建議。

_____

_____

【參考答案】

Physiologically, children have the primal instinct to cling to caretakers, seeking suggestions regarding basic areas of life in order to survive.

❹ 心理上，同儕的建議不可缺少，因為他們能幫助我們進行社交生活。

_____

_____

【參考答案】

Psychologically, suggestions from peers are indispensable since they help us with how to socialize in groups.

❺ 然而，當小孩成長為少年，我相信他們應該更常親自探索世界。

_____

_____

【參考答案】

Nevertheless, as children become adolescents, I believe they should venture into the world by themselves more frequently.

高分範文搶先看　▶ MP3 052

　　The two ways of learning about life as described in the statement carry various advantages depending on which stage of life we are in. I am inclined to hold the opinion that before one enters **adolescence**, he would explore the world more smoothly if given more advice from others, yet as one becomes a young adult, it is more beneficial to learn through personal experience.

　　First, it is easily **comprehensible** that from the moment our sense of self initially emerges in late **infancy** to the moment we begin forming our individual identity in late childhood, we rely on advice from not only elders but also our peers in order to develop normally both physical and mental. Physiologically, children have the **primal** instinct to cling to caretakers, seeking suggestions

　　題目敘述的兩種學習人生的方式都各有優點，端看我們處於哪個人生的階段。我傾向認為在少年期之前，如果多聽從他人建議，探索世界的過程會比較順利，然而當一個人成為年輕成人，透過親自體驗會比較有益處。

　　首先，不難理解的是從我們的自我意識在嬰兒期晚期萌芽，到兒童期晚期個人身份開始形成這段期間，我們不但依賴長輩，也依賴同儕的建議，為的是生理和心理方面都能正常發展。生理上，小孩有原始的本能要依附照顧者，為了生存而尋求關於生活基本面的建議。心理上，同儕的建議不可缺少，因為他們能幫助我們進

regarding basic areas of life in order to survive. Psychologically, suggestions from peers are indispensable since they help us with how to **socialize** in groups. Thus, the advantages of **imbibing** and applying advice in the early stage of growth cannot be overemphasized. To **fortify** my opinion, I would like to draw on the psychological theory, Maslow's hierarchy of needs, which **asserts** the needs for physiology, safety, and love/belonging form the fundamental levels of childhood development. Since children cannot provide for themselves, following suggestions from others will help protect them from **undesired** risks and satisfy the three levels of needs.

Nevertheless, as children become adolescents, I believe they should venture into the world by themselves more frequently.

行社交生活。因此，在成長初期，吸收並應用忠告的優點再怎麼強調都不為過。我想引用心理學理論，馬斯洛的需求階層，來加強我的看法。此理論主張對生理，安全和愛／歸屬感的三種需求形成兒童發展的基本層次。因為小孩無法照顧自己，遵循他人的建議能保護他們免於不必要的風險，並在基本需求的三個層次獲得滿足。

然而，當小孩成長為少年，我相信他們應該更常親自探索世界。健康的青少年應該培養自主能力，獨特的人格和

Healthy adolescents should cultivate **autonomy**, distinctive **dispositions** and **idiosyncrasies** which cannot be achieved if they seldom experience life personally. My point can be **validated** by taking the protagonist in the movie "Good Will Hunting" for example. Trapped mentally by his **traumatized** experience, Will Hunting, a 20-year-old man and physical abuse survivor, refuses to **exert** his genius for math and rejects **intimate** relationships. It is only after a psychologist unlocks his defense that Will embraces his true self and decides to embark on a journey to follow his soul mate. Hence, experiencing both joys and sorrow directly is crucial even for adults.

As for me, I definitely find experiencing everything firsthand **preferable**. Occasionally, firsthand experiences might induce frustration, yet the joy of **surmounting** frustration is incomparable.

特色，而如果他們鮮少親自體驗人生，這些都達不到。我的論點可由《心靈捕手》的主角為例獲得證實。二十歲的威爾·杭汀是身體虐待的倖存者，他被創傷經驗侷限，拒絕發揮數學天賦並排斥親密關係。只有在一位心理學家解開他的防衛後，威爾才擁抱真我，並決定展開追尋靈魂伴侶的旅程。因此，甚至對成人而言，直接體會愉悅和悲傷都是重要的。

我本人絕對偏好親自體驗人生的一切。偶爾，直接體會可能會導致挫折感，但克服挫折感的快樂是無法比擬的。

UNIT 07

正在消失的自然資源 — 搭配電影《阿凡達》（Avatar）

 WRITING TASK 2

TOPIC

"The world is losing lots of natural resources. Choose one resource that is disappearing and explain why it's urgent to save it." Use specific details and examples to support your viewpoint.

「這個世界正在失去許多自然資源。選擇一項正在消失的自然資源並解釋為何拯救這項資源是迫切的。」請使用精準的細節和例證支持你的論點。

單句中譯英

❶ 我們應該保護熱帶雨林，不只是為了生態保育，也是為了保護原住民族群，原住民族群的生活型態及文化跟熱帶雨林密不可分。

_____

_____

【參考答案】

We should save tropical rainforests for not only ecological preservation, but also the protection of indigenous peoples whose cultures are inseparable from the tropical rainforests.

❷ 熱帶雨林在穩定水循環、減少溫室氣體是不可或缺的，它同時提供地球上超過 50%的植物和動物物種的棲息地，並在人類世紀元提供關鍵的功能。

_____

_____

【參考答案】

Tropical rain forests are indispensable in stabilizing the water cycle and reducing greenhouse gases, and host over 50% of the plant and animal species on the earth, which serves a crucial function during the Anthropocene.

❸ 自從十九世紀工業化起始，溫室氣體總量已經達到前所未有的最高點，顯示了保護雨林的急迫性。

_____

_____

【參考答案】

Since the inception of industrialization in the 19th century, the amount of greenhouse gases has reached an unprecedented height, indicating the urgency to save rainforests.

❹ 沒有樹群吸收二氧化碳及產生氧氣,且 40%的氧氣是由熱帶雨林產生,溫室效應只會更劇烈惡化。

_____

_____

【參考答案】

Without trees to absorb carbon dioxide and generate oxygen, of which 40% is generated by tropical forests, the greenhouse effect will only deteriorate drastically.

❺ 例如,巴西政府正在建造世界上第三大的水壩,完成後將會淹沒亞馬遜雨林廣大的野生動物棲息地,並強迫四萬人牽移。

_____

_____

【參考答案】

For example, the Brazilian government is building the world's third largest dam, which will flood a vast wildlife habitat in the Amazon and force 40,000 residents to relocate.

⫽ 高分範文搶先看　▶ MP3 053

Among the natural resources that are being depleted by human activities, I believe that tropical rainforests are in dire need of preservation. We should save tropical rainforests for not only ecological preservation, but also the protection of **indigenous** peoples whose cultures are **inseparable** from the tropical rainforests.

Tropical rain forests are indispensable in **stabilizing** the water cycle and reducing greenhouse gases, and host over 50% of the plant and animal species on the earth, which serves a crucial function during the **Anthropocene**. Since the **inception** of industrialization in the 19th century, the amount of greenhouse gases has reached an **unprecedented** height, indicating

在被人類活動消耗的自然資源中，我相信熱帶雨林是需要迫切的保育。我們應該保護熱帶雨林，不只是為了生態保育，也是為了保護原住民族群，原住民族群的生活型態及文化跟熱帶雨林密不可分。

熱帶雨林在穩定水循環、減少溫室氣體是不可或缺的，它同時提供地球上超過 50%的植物和動物物種的棲息地，並在人類世紀元提供關鍵的功能。自從十九世紀工業化起始，溫室氣體總量已經達到前所未有的最高點，顯示了保護雨林的急迫性。然而，熱帶雨林的砍伐以驚人的速度正在進行，也剝奪了許多地棲物種的家。

Part 1 單句中英互譯

Part 2 段落中譯英

Part 3 精選大作文

287

the urgency to save rainforests. Yet, the **deforestation** of tropical rainforests is happening at an alarming rate, which has deprived numerous **terrestrial** species of their home. Without trees to absorb carbon dioxide and **generate** oxygen, of which 40% is generated by tropical forests, the greenhouse effect will only deteriorate drastically. With fewer trees to help maintain the **equilibrium** of the water cycle, humans will face more droughts.

Moreover, the destruction of tropical rain forests is as threatening as the **annihilation** of species in the movie, Avatar. The director of *Avatar*, James Cameron, has publicly acknowledged that the setting of the movie **mirrors** the Brazilian rainforest and that what happens in the movie is real to **numerous** indigenous peoples living there.

沒有樹群吸收二氧化碳及產生氧氣，且 40%的氧氣是由熱帶雨林產生，溫室效應只會更劇烈惡化。能幫助維持水循環平衡的樹減少了，人類未來將面對更多旱災。

此外，熱帶雨林的破壞就如同電影《阿凡達》裡的物種滅絕一樣令人感到威脅。《阿凡達》的導演詹姆士・克麥隆曾公開表示這部電影的場景呼應了巴西的雨林，而且電影裡發生的事對許多住在那裏的原住民族群而言是真實的。例如，巴西政府正在建造世界上第三大的水壩，完成後將會淹沒亞馬遜雨林廣大的野生動物

For example, the Brazilian government is building the world's third largest dam, which will flood a vast wildlife habitat in the Amazon and force 40,000 residents to relocate. Worse yet, uprooting the indigenous peoples from their homeland equals destroying their culture.

To conclude, tropical rainforests have been described by scientists as the lungs of the earth, and thus it is not difficult to **envisage** that just as **dysfunctional** human lungs will induce life-threatening peril, the massive destruction of tropical rainforests will cause a **devastating** effect on the earth.

棲息地，並強迫四萬人牽移。更糟糕的是，將原住民族群從他們的家鄉連根拔起等同於摧毀他們的文化。

　　總而言之，熱帶雨林被科學家描述為地球的肺，因此不難想像正如同功能失調的肺會導致威脅生命的危險，對熱帶雨林的大量破壞將導致地球上毀滅性的效應。

UNIT 08

環境類：保育瀕臨絕種動物的環境 — 搭配電影：《快樂腳》（Happy Feet）

 WRITING TASK 2

TOPIC

"Developing an industry is more important than saving the environment for endangered animals." Do you agree or disagree with the statement? Use specific details and examples to support your viewpoint.

「發展一項產業比保護瀕臨絕種動物的環境重要。」你同意或不同意以上的敘述?使用精準的細節和例證支持你的偏好。

 單句中譯英

❶ 我不同意發展產業應該優先於保護瀕臨絕種動物的環境，因為我相信摧毀自然環境最終會讓人類付出代價。

_____

_____

【參考答案】

I disagree with the view that developing an industry should take precedence over saving the environment for endangered species as I believe that destroying the natural environment will eventually take its toll on humans in the long run.

❷ 首先，考慮到北極熊和南極洲帝王企鵝的困境，就能得知破壞瀕臨絕種動物的環境明顯地導致人類磨難。

_____

_____

【參考答案】

First, the infliction on humans due to damaging the environment for endangered animals is conspicuous, considering the predicaments of polar bears in the Arctic and emperor penguins in Antarctica.

❸ 因為過去一世紀的急速工業化，全球暖化的現象已劇烈地惡化。

_____

_____

Part 1 單句中英互譯

Part 2 段落中譯英

Part 3 精選大作文

Due to rapid industrialization in the past century, global warming has been exacerbated drastically.

❹ 因此，由於北極冰層溶化，花較多時間在海裡狩獵的北極熊備受折磨，牠們被迫覓食時游更長的距離。

_____

_____

As a result, polar bears, which spend more time at sea hunting than on land, have suffered from the melting of Arctic ice, forcing them to swim for longer distances to search for food.

❺ 更糟糕的是，狩獵區域的縮減導致海豹減少，海豹是北極熊主要的獵物，而海豹減少也是受到漁業的影響。

_____

_____

What's worse, the shrinkage of the hunting area has caused the reduction of seals, polar bears' major prey, which is also affected by commercial overfishing.

▍高分範文搶先看　▶ MP3 054

The debate on the competition between economic development and the protection of endangered species has been going on for decades. I disagree with the view that developing an industry should take **precedence** over saving the environment for endangered species as I believe that destroying the natural environment will eventually take its toll on humans in the long run.

First, the **infliction** on humans due to damaging the environment for endangered animals is conspicuous, considering the **predicaments** of polar bears in **the Arctic** and emperor penguins in **Antarctica**. Due to rapid industrialization in the past century, global warming has been **exacerbated** drastically. As a result, polar bears, which spend

關於經濟發展及保護瀕臨絕種動物之爭辯已經持續了數十年。我不同意發展產業應該優先於保護瀕臨絕種動物的環境，因為我相信摧毀自然環境最終會讓人類付出代價。

首先，考慮到北極熊和南極洲帝王企鵝的困境，就能得知破壞瀕臨絕種動物的環境明顯地導致人類磨難。因為過去一世紀的急速工業化，全球暖化的現象已劇烈地惡化。因此，由於北極冰層溶化，花較多時間在海裡狩獵的北極熊備受折磨，牠們被迫覓食時游更長的距離。更糟糕的是，狩獵區域

more time at sea hunting than on land, have suffered from the melting of Arctic ice, forcing them to swim for longer distances to search for food. What's worse, the **shrinkage** of the hunting area has caused the reduction of seals, polar bears' major prey, which is also affected by commercial overfishing. If industries can take more actions to **alleviate** global warming, not only human's condition will be relieved by the decline of air pollution, but also marine ecology will be better **preserved**.

Furthermore, emperor penguins in Antarctica have been threatened by the fishing industry. Emperor penguins are not only deprived of their prey, fish and krill, but also are **jeopardized** by climate change, oil spills, and eco-tourism. The decrease of emperor penguins

的縮減導致海豹減少，海豹是北極熊主要的獵物，而海豹減少也是受到漁業的影響。如果產業能採取更多行動減緩全球暖化，不只人類生存的狀態會因為空污減少而獲得舒緩，海洋生態也能獲得更佳的保育。

此外，南極洲帝王企鵝一直遭受漁業威脅。不只帝王企鵝的獵物，魚和磷蝦，被剝奪了，帝王企鵝也因氣候變遷，漏油事件和生態觀光而陷入危險。直到《快樂腳》這部電影描繪一隻帝王企鵝展開旅程以找出為何魚量一直減少，帝王企鵝數量的減少才獲得大眾的

did not draw public attention until the movie, *Happy Feet*, featured an emperor penguin embarking upon a journey to find out why the fish were **dwindling**. The reason is exactly overfishing. The example indicates that the aforementioned industry harms endangered species, altering the food chain, which will eventually harm humans as we are at the top of the food chain.

Last but not least, since 70% of the earth is covered by oceans, if industries continue damaging marine ecology, it is not difficult to **envisage** a devastating future for the human environment. If we preserve the environment for endangered animals, humans might live with them **reciprocally**.

注意。原因就是過量捕魚。這個例子顯示上述產業傷害瀕臨絕種的動物，改變了食物鏈，而最終將會傷害人類，因為我們處於食物鏈的最頂端。

最後，既然地球的 70%的表面被海洋覆蓋，如果產業繼續損害海洋生態，不難想像出一個對人類環境而言，毀滅性的未來。如果我們保育瀕臨絕種動物的環境，人類可能與動物可以互惠共存。

UNIT 09

環境類：人類活動是否改善環境─搭配電影《永不妥協》與名人故事：麥特‧戴蒙

 WRITING TASK 2

TOPIC

"Some people believe human activities are harmful to the earth; others think human activities make the earth a better place. What is your opinion?" Use specific details and examples to support your viewpoint.

「有人相信人類活動對地球有害;而其他人認為人類活動讓地球成為更好的地方。」你的意見為何?請使用精準的細節和例證支持你的論點。

單句中譯英

❶ 但是我相信人類正使地球變成更美好的地方，因為我們有自我救贖的能力。

_____

_____

【參考答案】

Yet, I believe humans are making the world a more promising place because we are capable of self-redemption.

❷ 工業化已經摧毀了大自然，使眾多物種陷入瀕臨絕種的危機，且造成全球暖化惡化，然而，也有另一股反作用力致力於改善環境。

_____

_____

【參考答案】

Whereas industrialization has destroyed the wilderness, endangered numerous species, and exacerbated global warming, there is also a counterforce that strives to improve the environment.

❸ 在發現 PG&E 使用致癌化學物質並汙染加州辛克利地區的地下水之後，艾琳‧波洛克維奇和雇用她的律師事務所提出告訴，並贏了對抗 PG&E 的官司，不只協助當地居民獲得數百萬美金的賠償，也讓汙染區域或得修復。

_____

_____

【參考答案】

After finding out that PG&E used carcinogenic chemicals that contaminated groundwater in Hinkley, California, Brockovich and the law firm she worked for built and won the lawsuit against PG&E, not only helping the residents receive millions in compensation, but also leading to the remediation of contaminated areas.

❹ 只要有像波洛克維奇這樣關心他人痛苦的人士，人類對地球的損害就有被修復的希望。

_____

_____

【參考答案】

As long as there are people who like, Brockovich, care about others' suffering, there is hope that human damage to the world can be amended.

❺ 平民對損害地球環境的大財團做出的抗爭可能過於吃力，然而，要使地球更好我們不用捨近求遠。

_____

_____

【參考答案】

While civilians' fight against conglomerates that have conducted activities harmful to the earth might seem overwhelming, we don't have to look too far for the opportunity to make the world a better place.

▍高分範文搶先看　▶ MP3 055

Never before has the earth been altered so dramatically by human activities. Yet, I believe humans are making the world a more promising place because we are capable of self-**redemption**.

Whereas **industrialization** has destroyed the wilderness, endangered numerous species, and **exacerbated** global warming, there is also a **counterforce** that strives to improve the environment. The improvement is often propelled by those with a moral **conscience** that assumes responsibility for the well-being of humanity, which is **exemplified** by the story of Erin Brockovich, an American environmental activist, who became a household name after her antipollution lawsuit against Pacific Gas & Electric (PG&E) was adapted into a

人類活動未曾對地球造成今日般如此劇烈的改變。但是我相信人類正使地球變成更美好的地方，因為我們有自我救贖的能力。

工業化已經摧毀了大自然，使眾多物種陷入瀕臨絕種的危機，且造成全球暖化惡化，然而，也有另一股反作用力致力於改善環境。改善環境的力量往往被擁有道德良知的人士及隨之而來對人類福祉的責任感所推動。艾琳・波洛克維奇的故事即是例證，她是美國的環保運動人士，在她對 PG&E 提出的反污染官司被改編成好萊塢電影後，她成為家喻戶曉的名人。在發現 PG&E 使用致癌化學物質並汙染加州辛克利地區的地下水之後，艾琳・波洛克維奇和雇用她的

Hollywood movie. After finding out that PG&E used **carcinogenic** chemicals that **contaminated** groundwater in Hinkley, California, Brockovich and the law firm she worked for built and won the lawsuit against PG&E, not only helping the residents receive millions in **compensation**, but also leading to the **remediation** of contaminated areas. As long as there are people who like, Brockovich, care about others' suffering, there is hope that human damage to the world can be amended.

律師事務所提出告訴，並贏了對抗 PG&E 的官司，不只協助當地居民獲得數百萬美金的賠償，也讓汙染區域或得修復。只要有像波洛克維奇這樣關心他人痛苦的人士，人類對地球的損害就有被修復的希望。

While civilians' fight against **conglomerates** that have conducted activities harmful to the earth might seem overwhelming, we don't have to look too far for the opportunity to make the world a better place. Taking the daily necessity, water, for example. The global water

平民對損害地球環境的大財團做出的抗爭可能過於吃力，然而，要使地球更好我們不用捨近求遠。以日常所需的水為例，全球水資源危機和氣候變遷，生態破壞及赤貧現象有錯綜複雜的關係。為了使水資源的取得平等化，麥特・戴蒙和蓋瑞・懷特共同成立了

crisis is **intricately** interconnected with climate change, ecological destruction and extreme poverty. To equalize water resource access, Matt Damon and Gary White cofounded a charity, Water.org, which builds water and sanitation facilities in **destitute** regions, proving that human existence can be elevated by a single act of **philanthropy.**

While it is debatable whether human activities generate positive or negative impacts, I maintain that the earth is being **meliorated** with continuous philanthropic and environmental campaigns.

Water.org 慈善機構，Water.org 在赤貧地區建造取水和衛生設施，證明了單一慈善行動能提升人類生存的狀態。

人類活動是否造成正面或負面影響仍可辯論，但我認為隨著持續的慈善及環保運動，地球正持續被改善。

Part 1 單句中英互譯

Part 2 段落中譯英

Part 3 精選大作文

擁有財富即是成功？ — 搭配名人故事：德雷莎修女（Mother Teresa）與瑪拉拉尤瑟夫扎依（Malala Yousafzai）

WRITING TASK 2

TOPIC

"Only people who possess a large amount of wealth are successful". Do you agree or disagree with the statement? Use specific details and examples to support your viewpoint.

「擁有許多財富的人才是成功的。」你同意或不同意以上的敘述?使用精準的細節和例證支持你的論點。

🎓 單句中譯英

❶ 在資本主義社會，擁有大量財富似乎是成功的主要指標。

_____

_____

【參考答案】

In a capitalist society, owning a large amount of wealth seems to be the prime sign of success.

❷ 流行文化是如此地推崇富裕者以至於有錢人已經變成新的貴族。

_____

_____

【參考答案】

Popular culture exalts the rich so much so that the rich have become the new royalty.

❸ 我確信一個人對他的所作所為是否保持熱誠才是關鍵。

_____

_____

【參考答案】

My firm belief is that whether one has passion for what he does is the key.

❹ 我的看法呼應艾伯特・史懷哲的名言。艾伯特・史懷哲是 1952 年的

諾貝爾和平獎得主，他曾說「成功不是達到幸福的關鍵。幸福才是達到成功的關鍵。」

_____

_____

【參考答案】

My opinion resonates with Albert Schweitzer's famous saying. Albert Schweitzer, the recipient of the Nobel Peace Prize in 1952, once said, "Success is not the key to happiness. Happiness is the key to success."

❺ 將熱誠轉化為行動能帶來成就感。反之，只有錢並不能保證幸福感；充其量這只是華而不實，遲早會崩解的成功表相。

_____

_____

【參考答案】

Actualizing passion into action will induce a sense of fulfillment; instead, merely owning money is no guarantee for felicity; at best, it's a meretricious facade of success that will disintegrate sooner or later.

高分範文搶先看　▶ MP3 056

In a capitalist society, owning a large amount of wealth seems to be the prime sign of success. Popular culture **exalts** the rich so much so that the rich have become the new royalty. Yet, if one **delves** into the **constituents** of success, he is likely to discover that money alone can hardly satisfy those elements, which is why I disagree with the statement.

My firm belief is that whether one has passion for what he does is the key. My opinion **resonates** with Albert Schweitzer's famous saying. Albert Schweitzer, the recipient of the Nobel Peace Prize in 1952, once said, "Success is not the key to happiness. Happiness is the key to success. If you love what you are doing, you will be successful." If a person's life-long pursuit is aimed at **accumulating**

在資本主義社會，擁有大量財富似乎是成功的主要指標。流行文化是如此地推崇富裕者以至於有錢人已經變成新的貴族。然而，如果一個人深入探討成功的元素，他很可能會發現財富幾乎不可能滿足那些元素，這正是我不同意題目敘述的原因。

我確信一個人對他的所作所為是否保持熱誠才是關鍵。我的看法呼應艾伯特‧史懷哲的名言。艾伯特‧史懷哲是 1952 年的諾貝爾和平獎得主，他曾說「成功不是達到幸福的關鍵。幸福才是達到成功的關鍵。如果你熱愛你做的事，你就會成功」。若一個人終生追求的目標是盡量累積財富，他注定會活得像小氣財神。小氣

as much wealth as possible, he is bound to lead a life like Scrooge, the protagonist in Charles Dickens' novel, *A Christmas Carol*, who is miserly and has no passion in his life. **Actualizing** passion into action will induce a sense of **fulfillment**; instead, merely owning money is no guarantee for **felicity**; at best, it's a **meretricious** facade of success that will **disintegrate** sooner or later.

Furthermore, the achievements of most public figures who are deemed successful globally are rarely **ascribed** to their wealth. While the examples of such figures abound, I would take two prominent figures, Mother Teresa and Malala Yousafzai as examples. It goes without saying that the former's success arose from her selfless devotion to the **destitute** and the ill in India, and

財神是查爾斯·狄更斯的小說《聖誕頌歌》的主角,他很吝嗇,而且人生中沒有熱誠。將熱誠轉化為行動能帶來成就感。反之,只有錢並不能保證幸福感;充其量這只是華而不實,遲早會崩解的成功表相。

此外,大部分在全球都被視為成功者的那些公眾人物,他們的成就很少被歸因於財富。這種人物的例子非常多,而我舉兩位著名人物為例,德雷莎修女和馬拉拉·尤瑟夫札伊。無庸置疑地,前者的成功來自她在印度對貧苦及生病民眾的無私奉獻,而後者的成功來自她對兒童的,尤其是女性的受教權的倡導。馬拉拉,巴基斯坦的女權運動者,是有史

the latter 's arose from her advocacy for children's, especially girls' right of education. Malala, the Pakistani female rights activist, is the youngest ever Nobel Peace Prize **laureate**, having accepted the Nobel Peace Prize at age 17 in 2014. It is **conspicuous** that their success is not relevant to their possession of **opulence**.

The above examples demonstrate that success solely built upon wealth is hardly universally recognized. Those unquestionably **acknowledged** to be successful are people who are **passionately** committed to what they do.

以來最年輕的諾貝爾和平獎得主，在 2014 年她十七歲時得到此獎。很明顯地，他們的成功和他們擁有的財富毫無關係。

以上例證顯示只建構在財富之上的成功很難被普世認可。無疑地，被認為是成功人士的是那些對所作所為保持熱誠的人。

Part 1 單句中英互譯

Part 2 段落中譯英

Part 3 精選大作文

UNIT 11

人生觀：取得成功應具備的特質 — 搭配名人故事：李安與歐普拉·溫佛瑞

WRITING TASK 2

TOPIC

"In your opinion, what are the crucial characteristics that one must have to achieve success in life?" Use specific details and examples to support your
viewpoint.

「你認為一個人要達到成功需具備哪些重要的特質？」你同意或不同意以上的敘述？請使用精準的細節和例證支持你的論點。

🎓 單句中譯英

❶ 明顯地，渴望成功是人性的一部分，就我個人而言，有四個為了取得成功不可缺少的特質，即正向意圖、瞭解自己的才華、相信自己及努力。

_____

_____

【參考答案】

Evidently, it is part of human nature to aspire to succeed, and personally, four characteristics stand out as indispensable traits to attain success, namely positive intention, knowing one's gift, belief in oneself, and making efforts.

❷ 在物質化的社會，成功常跟擁有財富混淆，因此大部分的人忽略了追求成功的動機。

_____

_____

【參考答案】

In a materialistic society, success is often misidentified with the possession of wealth, and thus most people disregard the motivation for their pursuit.

❸ 歐普拉‧溫佛瑞就是依賴正向意圖驅策她成功的名人。歐普拉‧溫佛瑞是億萬富翁及媒體大亨。

_____

_____

【參考答案】

A renowned person who relies on positive intention as an impetus for her success is Oprah Winfrey, a billionaire and a media mogul.

❹ 另一位展現這項特色的名人是李安，他是兩次奧斯卡金像獎最佳導演獎的得主，李安在青少年時期就發現自己有寫劇本的才華。

_____

_____

【參考答案】

Another celebrity who demonstrates this feature is Ang Lee, two-time winner of the Academy Award for Best Director, who discovered his gift for writing scripts during adolescence.

❺ 然而，如果不相信自己和缺乏堅持不懈的努力，以上所提的特質都不會具體化為成就。

_____

_____

【參考答案】

However, the aforementioned traits will not be actualized into attainment without belief in oneself and making perseverant efforts.

高分範文搶先看　▶ MP3 057

There are many **motivational** speakers in every country that impart the secrets of success to the public. Evidently, it is part of human nature to aspire to succeed, and personally, four **characteristics** stand out as indispensable traits to attain success, namely positive intention, knowing one's gift, belief in oneself, and making efforts.

Positive intention is the driving force behind success. In a materialistic society, success is often **misidentified** with the **possession** of wealth, and thus most people disregard the motivation for their pursuit. Nonetheless, I don't think that success will be **justifiable** without positive intention. A **renowned** person who relies on positive intention as an **impetus** for her

每個國家都有許多勵志演說家向大眾傳授成功的祕訣。明顯地，渴望成功是人性的一部分，就我個人而言，有四個為了取得成功不可缺少的特質，即正向意圖、瞭解自己的才華、相信自己及努力。

正向意圖是成功的驅策力。在物質化的社會，成功常跟擁有財富混淆，因此大部分的人忽略了追求成功的動機。然而，我認為缺乏正向意圖，成功不會有正當性。歐普拉・溫佛瑞就是依賴正向意圖驅策她成功的名人。歐普拉・溫佛瑞是億萬富翁及媒體大亨。在 1990 年代，當大部分的談話性節目都製作充滿衝突的內容，

success is Oprah Winfrey, a billionaire and a media **mogul**. In the 1990s, while most talk shows produced **confrontational** content, Winfrey boldly changed the style of her talk show to the one that was based on positive intention. Besides, Winfrey found her gift for communication early, as she started working in a radio station at 16. Knowing one's gift is one of the most **salient** characteristics of successful people. Another celebrity who demonstrates this feature is Ang Lee, two- time winner of the Academy Award for Best Director, who discovered his gift for writing scripts during **adolescence**.

However, the aforementioned traits will not be **actualized** into **attainment** without belief in oneself and making perseverant efforts. Both Winfrey and Lee under went experiences of

溫佛瑞大膽地將她的談話性節目的風格改變成以正向意圖為出發點。此外，當溫佛瑞十六歲開始在廣播電台工作時，早就發現她對溝通的才華。瞭解自我的才華是成功人士最顯著的特色之一。另一位展現這項特色的名人是李安，他是兩次奧斯卡金像獎最佳導演獎的得主，李安在青少年時期就發現自己有寫劇本的才華。

然而，如果不相信自己和缺乏堅持不懈的努力，以上所提的特質都不會具體化為成就。溫佛瑞和李安都有不被肯定的經驗，這些經驗原本可能動搖他們發展才華的決心，但

invalidation, which might have **swayed** their determination to develop their talents, yet they believed in themselves despite others' disapproval. Ang Lee has written about his struggle of being a stay-at-home father and having his scripts constantly rejected. Winfrey described how she was **invalidated** because of her gender and ethnic identity. Also, they had **persevered** in making endeavors for decades before acquiring their success. I believe that **endeavor** is the key; without efforts, the other characteristics will hardly impel any achievement.

To sum up, among the four features, continuous endeavors should be the universally acknowledged key feature.

是儘管別人不認同，他們還是相信自己。李安曾經描寫他以往當家庭主夫及劇本不斷被退回等掙扎。溫佛瑞曾描述她因性別和種族身份而不被肯定。而且，他們在獲得成功前，堅持不懈地努力，長達數十年。我相信努力是關鍵，沒有努力，其他的特質很難激發任何成就。

總而言之，這四個特質中，持續努力應該是普世公認的關鍵特質。

UNIT 12

人們不滿足於現狀 —— 搭配電影
《命運好好玩》（Click）

WRITING TASK 2

TOPIC

"People nowadays are rarely content with the present; they always aim higher or desire more." Do you agree or disagree with the statement? Use specific details and examples to support your viewpoint.

「當今的人們很少滿足於現狀。他們總是將目標訂得更高或想要更多。」你同意或不同意以上敘述？請使用精準的細節和例證支持你的論點。

單句中譯英

❶ 住在資本化和競爭激烈社會的人們都傾向要出人頭地。

_____

_____

【參考答案】

Those living in a capitalist and competitive society tend to follow the path to climb the social ladder.

❷ 然而，在物質化的社會，許多人將他們個人的價值依附在物質財產上，因為層出不窮的廣告會洗腦消費者去做更多消費。

_____

_____

【參考答案】

Nonetheless, in a materialistic society, many people attach their individual values to material possessions due to incessant commercials that brainwash consumers into buying more.

❸ 轎車和手機的廣告常和幸福感或社會高階地位連結，向消費者暗示如果他們擁有那些產品，他們就離幸福或高社會地位更近一步。

_____

_____

【參考答案】

Commercials of cars and cell phones are often connected with a sense of felicity or indication of elevated social status, implying to consumers that if they possess the products, they are one step closer to happiness or high status.

❹ 但是，這只是行銷策略創造的海市蜃樓，藉此誘惑消費者花更多錢，但消費者從不感覺滿足，因為新產品總是快速推出。

【參考答案】

However, this is only a mirage created by marketing strategies to lure consumers into spending more, but never feeling satisfied since new products are launched rapidly.

❺ 因此，從物質主義尋求快樂的人們會陷於想要更多，而欲望只能暫時被滿足的惡性循環。

【參考答案】

Thus, people who seek happiness from materialism are trapped in the vicious cycle of desiring more and having their desires satisfied only temporarily.

高分範文搶先看　▶ MP3 058

Those living in a **capitalist** and competitive society tend to follow the path to climb the social ladder. While desiring more might induce positive or negative effects, I am inclined to agree with the statement.

First, it is part of human nature to want more. Nonetheless, in a **materialistic** society, many people attach their individual values to material possessions due to **incessant** commercials that **brainwash** consumers into buying more. Commercials of cars and cell phones are often connected with a sense of **felicity** or indication of **elevated** social status, implying to consumers that if they possess the products, they are one step closer to happiness or high status. However, this is only a **mirage** created by marketing strategies to

住在資本化和競爭激烈社會的人們都傾向要出人頭地。想要更多可能導致正面或負面的效應，但我傾向同意題目敘述。

首先，想要更多是人性的一部份。然而，在物質化的社會，許多人將他們個人的價值依附在物質財產上，因為層出不窮的廣告會洗腦消費者去做更多消費。轎車和手機的廣告常和幸福感或社會高階地位連結，向消費者暗示如果他們擁有那些產品，他們就離幸福或高社會地位更近一步。但是，這只是行銷策略創造的海市蜃樓，藉此誘惑消費者花更多錢，但消費者從不感覺滿足，因為新產品總是快速推出。因此，從物質主義尋求

lure consumers into spending more, but never feeling satisfied since new products are launched rapidly. Thus, people who seek happiness from **materialism** are trapped in the **vicious** cycle of desiring more and having their desires satisfied only **temporarily**.

Secondly, as most of us belonging to the **bourgeoisie** climb the social ladder, it is difficult to strike a balance between family and work. While we are constantly **swamped** by work demands, we forget to pause and remind ourselves to **appreciate** what we already have. Examples abound that many men already have **affectionate** families, yet they still desire more power or wealth, which is portrayed in the movie, *Click*. The protagonist in *Click* is a **workaholic** who keeps ignoring his family as he strives to meet the demands

快樂的人們會陷於想要更多，而欲望只能暫時被滿足的惡性循環。

第二，當大多數屬於中產階級的我們在社會上力爭上游時，很難在家庭和工作間取得平衡。當我們不斷被工作要求淹沒時，我們會忘記暫停一下並提醒自己體會已經擁有的事物。很多例子顯示許多人已經有摯愛他們的家人，但仍渴望更多權力或財富，電影《命運好好玩》描繪了這現象。《命運好好玩》的主角是個工作狂，當他努力要達到老闆的要求及成為公司合夥人的目標時，他一直忽略他的家庭。最終，由於一個神奇遙控器掌控了他的世界，他對人生失去控制，雖然他原本想要用這遙控

from his boss and his goal to make partner in his company. He ultimately pays the price of losing his family as his life **spiraled** out of control due to a magic remote control that overtakes his universe, though initially he intends to use the remote to fast forward the time to his promotion.

In conclusion, it has become a social norm to be discontent and aspire more, which, when developed to the extreme, might place us in the predicament as symbolized by the **metaphorical** remote in *Click*.

器將時間快轉到他升遷的時刻，他也付出失去家人的代價。

總而言之，不滿足並渴望更多已經變成社會常態，當這現象發展至極端時，可能會讓我們處於像《命運好好玩》裡的遙控器隱喻象徵的困境。

Part 1 單句中英互譯

Part 2 段落中譯英

Part 3 精選大作文

國家圖書館出版品預行編目(CIP)資料

雅思寫作聖經：大作文 / Amanda Chou著.
-- 初版. --新北市：倍斯特出版事業有限公司,
2021.11　面；　公分. -- (考用英語系列；
031) ISBN 978-986-06095-7-8 (平裝)
1.國際英語語文測驗系統　2.作文

805.189　　　　　　　　　　　　110017284

考用英語系列　034

雅思寫作聖經-大作文（英式發音 附QR Code音檔）

初　　版　　2021年11月
定　　價　　新台幣460元

作　　者　　Amanda Chou
出　　版　　倍斯特出版事業有限公司
發 行 人　　周瑞德
電　　話　　886-2-8245-6905
傳　　真　　886-2-2245-6398
地　　址　　23558 新北市中和區立業路83巷7號4樓
E - m a i l　　best.books.service@gmail.com
官　　網　　www.bestbookstw.com
總 編 輯　　齊心瑀
特約編輯　　陳韋佑
封面構成　　高鍾琪
內頁構成　　菩薩蠻數位文化有限公司
印　　製　　大亞彩色印刷製版股份有限公司

港澳地區總經銷　　泛華發行代理有限公司
地　　　　址　　香港新界將軍澳工業邨駿昌街7號2樓
電　　　　話　　852-2798-2323
傳　　　　真　　852-3181-3973